Revel: Twelve Dancing Princesses Retold

DEMELZA CARLTON

Book 4 in the Romance a Medieval Fairy Tale series

This is a work of fiction. Names, characters, businesses, places, events and incidents are either the products of the author's imagination or used in a fictitious manner. Any resemblance to actual persons, living or dead, or actual events is purely coincidental.

Copyright © 2017 Demelza Carlton

Lost Plot Press

All rights reserved.

ISBN-13: 978-0-9922693-8-8

ISBN-10: 0-9922693-8-5

DEDICATION

For all those who have given their lives fighting for
what they believed in..

One

"We should have made the wedding this week," Dokia said, lacing her fingers through Vasco's. "Waiting eight more days is torture."

"I call it delicious anticipation," Vasco replied. "Besides, if we got married this week, we wouldn't have a house to live in. Tomorrow I'll make a start on the roof, so that when you become my bride, we'll be able to spend our wedding night under a roof."

She lifted her gaze to the sky and sighed. "Right now, I would be perfectly happy with the stars as my roof, the night I become yours. If I have you, I will have everything I ever wanted."

"Right up until it rains," Vasco said.

Dokia laughed. "And that is why you're my lord and provider, or you will be, after next week. I cannot think of rain while the sun still shines."

"Ah, but the sun is setting now. And once the sun is gone, I'll make sure that all you can think about is you and me." Vasco raced into the trees, pulling her along until they reached the clearing they had claimed as their own.

Kissing Dokia was like air – he couldn't get enough of her. Their kisses grew more heated, and their clothes began to loosen before they started removing them entirely.

Vasco laid her on the soft grass by the stream, where she gazed up at him with eyes full of love.

"With all the practice we're getting, you will be perfect at this when our wedding night comes," she teased.

"Only because you are already perfect, my Eudocia," Vasco said, kicking off his boots.

"Flatterer," she replied, undoing the lacing of her gown to expose most of her chest. "What about these? Perfect enough for you?"

"Too perfect for me," Vasco replied. "Much like the rest of you. I don't know what madness made you accept me, but before you recover your senses, I will accept anything you offer me."

She parted her gown completely, laying herself bare. "I offer you everything I am, and everything I have. Take me, Vasco."

Vasco opened his mouth to respond, but another voice cut in, "That's a mighty pretty morsel. Too pretty for some peasant boy."

Something crashed into the side of Vasco's head and he fell lifeless to the grass. He never heard Dokia's screams pierce the air, or those from the village as it burned. When he awoke, there was nothing but silence and death to greet him.

For hours he walked the ruins of his home, looking for hope where there was none. So he did what any young man would after everything he had known was dead and buried: he joined the army, figuring that death would find him soon enough.

But fate had a different plan for Vasco.

Two

Wishing to be the fairest of them all was the worst kind of curse to visit on a princess, Bianca mused. She alone among her sisters had fair hair, so pale that in today's bright sunlight it almost seemed white. It made her stand out, drawing unwanted attention from men and women alike. The men she did not mind so much, for she knew that as a princess she was near untouchable to most of them, but when the queen's gaze landed on her one too many times, nothing good could come of it. That Bianca was the daughter of a minor concubine, a princess in name, but not much more, who outshone the queen's own daughter, only made it worse.

So that was why the fairest of all the king's daughters now rode through the unseasonable heat into exile at the Summer Palace. A place where the king's virgin daughters would be safe, the queen had said with a vicious smile, until they were married.

Bianca knew better. The Summer Palace was where girls were sent to become old maids. No girl who had ever been sent there had returned, nor had they received word of any fortuitous marriage alliances the girls had made. That in itself was suspicious, Bianca mused. For the proposed marriage between the queen's daughter, Lagle, and the neighbouring king had been trumpeted far and wide. For one horrible moment, Bianca had worried that she would be sent as Lagle's companion to the foreign court, but the queen had taken a dislike to another minor princess instead. So poor Ava could look forward to a lifetime of servitude, while Bianca was granted the relative freedom of exile.

Right now, though, Bianca almost envied Ava. Ava would ride through shady forest all the way to her new home, while Bianca's road was just that…a road. A road tramped by thousands of marching feet, when her father's armies had been fighting to claim this place, and it was kept clear to facilitate troop movements, should they be needed in future. So the sun beat down mercilessly, with no shelter in sight.

Which brought her back to the curse of being the fairest of all the king's daughters. Her cheeks burned, though she had no reason to blush. Bianca had never experienced a sunburn before, but if this was one, she had no desire to experience one again. By the time they reached the edge of a wood and a cottage where she might take shelter, Bianca's face felt like it was on fire. She signalled for her guards to halt, and she dismounted. Praying that the owner of the cottage was home and willing to offer temporary shelter to a traveller, Bianca knocked tentatively at the door.

The door creaked open, as though she was expected. "Princess!" an elderly voice croaked. "Please, come inside." A wrinkled hand beckoned her in.

Bianca glanced at her guards, who didn't look concerned, so she accepted the old woman's invitation and followed her into the blessed cool of the cottage.

The old woman shuffled to the table where she poured two cups of liquid from a stoppered jug. Then she waved her hand and the door slammed shut. That got Bianca's attention. "I am Kun, the witch who guards these lands. Welcome, princess. I take it you're not accustomed to travel?"

Bianca shook her head, wincing as this only seemed to make her face hurt more.

"I can give you a salve to soothe that burn, if you wish. If you're anything like your sisters, you wish to stay pretty for as long as possible." She gave a gummy grin.

"I would prefer not to be pretty," Bianca said with regret. "Pretty princesses attract unwanted attention. Much better to be unseen."

The woman cackled again. "An invisible princess, eh? That's quite a trick. Even more impressive than the day when the queen's new gown…"

"Please don't mention that," Bianca groaned. "I only wished to see how the queen's new gown was made. I had no idea what was invisible to me became invisible to everyone else, too. My mother banned me from using magic every day after that, so that the queen would not know that it was I who made her gown invisible so that she appeared naked at court. I think she suspect something, though. She has never liked me."

Kun patted Bianca's hand. "It matters not. You're far from court and the queen now, and your mother, too, I think. Mayhap you should practice your magic a little more. You never know when it might be useful to become invisible."

If Bianca didn't know better, she would think Kun knew of her desire to escape. Or perhaps Kun knew the truth about life in the Summer Palace. Surely the politics could not be worse than those in the king's harem. But where there were a lot of women… "Are there many ladies residing at the Summer Palace?" she ventured.

"Not so many. With you, there shall be twelve princesses. All about your age, and ripe for marriage. All they need are suitable husbands."

Bianca tried to hide her surprise. What, no old maids? Were the stories wrong, and the girls really would be married off? Or were the old maids taken somewhere else?

"Here's your salve," Kun said. The jar clattered to the table from her shaking hands. "You be sure to put some on now, then another coat morning and night. It should heal without a blemish."

Bianca obeyed. The salve seemed to extinguish the flames, though some of the heat remained. "Thank you," she said with feeling.

"You can come visit, any time you wish to practice your magic," Kun said.

"I… I can leave the palace? To come and visit you?" Bianca asked in surprise.

Kun snorted. "It is a palace, child, not a prison. Within the borders you will be safe. My cottage marks the edge of palace lands, so take care you do not go beyond it. The Summer Palace has its pleasures, as I'm sure you will find out, once you begin to explore. No doubt your sisters will enlighten you."

Her sisters. Bianca swallowed. Half sisters, more

like. And her rivals, should her father choose to marry one of them off for an alliance. Marriage would be her only means of escape, and if the opportunity arose, Bianca intended to take it. Perhaps being the fairest of them all might not be a curse, in this case.

Three

When Bianca left Kun's cottage, she found her guards had gone. Her mare stood outside where she'd left her, along with the packhorses carrying her belongings, but no one else. When Bianca looked askance at Kun, the old woman just grinned.

"Like I said, princess, you are safe here. There is no need for guards, while you are on the grounds of the Summer Palace."

Bianca looked around nervously. "But I do not yet know where the Summer Palace is," she said.

The old woman cackled. "Neither did your guards, for none of them have been allowed to go further up the road than my cottage." She eyed Bianca. "Simply follow the road. It will lead you to your destination."

"Is it far?" Bianca asked, hating the tremor in her voice. Her instincts told her to turn her horse in the opposite direction and urge it to a gallop until she was as far away from this place as possible.

"Less than an hour's ride, I am told. But that depends on just how eager you are to reach the palace."

Bianca swallowed. Perhaps Kun truly could read her mind.

Bianca found that for a less than eager princess, on a tired mount she had no desire to kick into a faster pace than a walk, it was indeed less than an hour before the palace loomed into view. Much smaller than the women's palace in the capital, she would not have called it a palace at all, if not for the decorative stonework that marked it as a noble's residence. Her father's seal on the gate left no question as to her destination. Small though it was, this was the Summer Palace, and her home for the foreseeable future. But not, she vowed, the rest of her life.

Servants ran out to greet her, to take care of her horses and see to her things. None of them dared raise their gaze to meet the eyes of a princess. That was as it should be, Bianca supposed. Then why did she feel such a strong burst of fear from them all? Perhaps she only imagined it.

"Princess Bianca, I presume?" a booming male voice rang out, preceding a richly dressed man who bowed low before her. "I am Efe, cousin to the queen, and the steward of the Summer Palace. The king wouldn't trust anyone less with such treasured jewels from his harem such as yourself and your sisters."

A crow cawed loudly with what sounded like laughter as it took flight from the roof above.

Bianca drew herself up to her haughtiest height, which sadly fell short of this odious man's shoulder. Nevertheless, she was a princess and the king's daughter, not merely some distant relation of the queen's. "No, he would not trust a lesser noble then yourself," she said sweetly. "After all, guard duty for a group of women who are used to living a protected life in the palace is hardly a job for someone the king values highly."

The steward's nostrils flared. Her barb had indeed landed. "I would not expect such a sheltered princess as yourself to know anything of the dangers outside your father's palace in the capital." His vulpine grin said what his words did not: that he hoped Bianca would fall afoul of some of these dangers, for he would enjoy her misfortune.

Bianca suppressed a snort, for such things were unladylike. She was no ordinary princess, but let the man believe what he liked. She had learned politics from her very infancy, for no girl survived long in a harem otherwise. Let him do his worst. She would be prepared. Bianca bowed her head to hide her smile.

The steward seemed to take this as submission. More fool him. "I shall take you to your quarters, and to see your sisters." He waved her inside.

For a moment, Bianca hesitated on the threshold. Even in the evening light, it seemed much brighter outside the confines of the Summer Palace. But such fears were silly, she told herself. Taking a deep breath, she strode forward with her head held high.

Four

Bianca heard her sisters before she saw them. The sounds of women at dinner when there were no men to command restraint was a familiar song of home. Lesser wives, concubines and their daughters who didn't have the status to be entitled to a private apartment had shared a common table in the harem. Several tables, as her father prided himself on the sheer number of women under his authority.

So it was with a smile on her lips that she entered the dining hall, taking a deep breath to greet her sisters.

Bianca's gaze swept across their faces and stopped dead.

She knew every face but one.

The ruddy face of a man beamed at her from under a hat so fluffy and floppy it looked like he wore a dead puppy on his head. If this was to be a new court fashion, Bianca was glad to be well away from it. "And who might you be?" the strange man slurred, raising a cup of wine to her.

Bianca lowered her eyes, but had to force herself not to incline her head. There could only be two men superior to a princess – her husband, and the king. As this man was neither, he must be beneath her notice. Her sisters didn't deem his question important enough to answer, either.

"This is Princess Bianca," Efe said. "Only just arrived from the palace." He made her sound like some sort of delectable dish, fresh from the kitchen.

Bianca suppressed a shiver. She'd heard children's tales of men who ate human flesh, but surely they were nothing but stories. Yet the way Efe spoke…

"You must sit beside me, princess, and tell me about your father's court," the man said.

As if by magic, her sisters slid up the bench to make space for her. For a moment, she hesitated, wondering what they knew about the stranger that she did not, but she could hardly ask them in front of the man. Better to ask him to talk about himself. Her mother and the other concubines had often said it was a man's favourite conversation topic, for the more he talked about himself, the more he liked the lady who pretended to listen.

But Bianca did not need to pretend. "I would much rather hear about you, sir. We hear little of the adventures to be had in the world outside my father's harem. The women's palace shelters us from such things. But you, I am sure, have travelled very far. How did you come here?"

He laughed so hard he spat out his wine. "By horse, of course! It isn't how I came here that matters, but why. Do you know why I am here, pretty princess?"

Bianca recognised the lust in his eyes. She lowered her gaze and shook her head. "I am just arrived, so I have not yet heard, sir."

"I am here to get myself a wife, and a palace!" he announced, grinning. The grin vanished when he reached for his wine, only to find Brenna's little dog lapping at the cup. "Wretched creature!" he shouted. The dog took fright and galloped across the table to seek refuge under Brenna's chair.

What appetite Bianca had possessed now vanished at the sight of dog footprints in every remaining platter of food. She waited for a maidservant to remove the tainted dishes, as would happen in the women's palace in the capital, but no one moved except the man beside her, who seized another chicken leg.

"More wine!" he called, raising his cup. "And a fresh cup to drink it from."

To Bianca's surprise, Hazel rose from her seat. "I will fetch it," she said, and headed out of the hall.

"You make my decision a difficult one," the man said. "Which of you will be my wife? If I can only have one of you, should I choose the prettiest, or the most obedient?"

Silence reigned at the table, broken only by the sound of mastication. No one laughed at his attempted jest, and none of them deigned to reply. Was that because they'd given up on the chance of escape from this life?

Bianca refused to give up, so she seized her chance. "You should choose the fairest, sir, the one who will best please you." She lowered her gaze and batted her eyelashes, as she'd seen the maids do to the handsome guards, when they thought no one else was looking. She felt like a complete fool, until she realised it had worked.

"You're as wise as you are beautiful, Princess Bianca," the man said. "I think you will please me very well."

Triumph welled up in her breast, but she did her best to hide it. "I hope so, sir."

Hazel returned with a goblet of wine, which she presented to the man. He drank it off in three huge gulps, then flashed a red-lipped smile at Hazel. "Thank you, my dear."

Bianca held her breath, but she caught the sneer that curled Hazel's lips. Hazel didn't want him for a husband.

He'd evidently caught her look of distaste, too. "But I think Princess Bianca is prettier than you. If she were to fetch me more wine, I think she will capture my heart completely."

"I will show her where to find it, then. Bianca?" Hazel jerked her head imperiously toward the door.

From princess to serving wench? Bianca balked at the thought, but she could do worse things to catch a husband and secure her escape from exile. Resignedly, she rose from the bench and followed Hazel out.

"Good girl," the man slurred behind her.

Bianca gritted her teeth. She would pay a high price for her escape if she were to marry that fool, whoever he was. But weren't all men fools?

<h1 style="text-align:center">Five</h1>

Bianca followed Hazel through the house to the wine cellar, which she was surprised to find appeared bigger than the house above.

It wasn't until they were deep between the dusty barrels that Hazel spoke. "You're wasting your time with that one," she said. "Like all the others, he'll be gone in three days."

"Others?" Bianca asked, her mind whirling. The thought of better men to choose from was certainly appealing.

Hazel grinned. "Oh, so many others. The promise of a palace and a princess's hand in marriage is quite the prize to a penniless adventurer, which most of them are. Dear Cousin Efe dresses them up in fancy clothes, but if you look closely, you can see how poorly they fit. Borrowed finery instead of the patched rags they arrive in, so that we allow them to sit at our table, but they will learn no secrets from us." She pointed at a barrel. "This is the one. This wine is stronger than anything you have ever tasted, which is why we don't. It's for men only, Cousin Efe says, which is fine by us. Here, look at the mark." She rapped her knuckle against the barrel, below a blackened smudge.

Bianca squinted at it. Now she looked more closely, she realised it was a brand, applied several times to the same barrel or just once by a particularly unsteady hand belonging to a man who'd perhaps drunk too much of his own wine. "Is it a bird of some kind?"

Hazel nodded. "This comes specially from somewhere far to the west. It's Efe's private supply, which is why we give it to his guests." She took a jug and proceeded to fill it from the barrel.

"Why didn't he dine with us tonight?" Bianca asked. Surely the queen's cousin would take every opportunity to dine with princesses, if only to make himself feel important.

Hazel laughed. "Oh, he wouldn't stoop to eat with us. We're the queen's hostages to our mothers' good behaviour. Anyone too pretty or too clever or even anyone who catches our father's eye for too long winds up here. For if another wife's daughters marry better than hers, she might lose her place as principal wife and queen. Perhaps that's why he forces us to share meals with beggars and soldiers of fortune, in the hope that we're silly enough to marry them. Disgraced daughters, disgraced mothers…that would only serve to cement her power in the capital."

Considering the idea, Bianca shook her head. "More likely she intends to leave us here to rot in spinsterhood, for any children we might have would still possess royal blood, no matter who their father was. But why would that man tonight think he had a chance to marry one of us, if he is a beggar?"

Hazel winked. "Delusions of grandeur, I'm sure. He believes he is better than any man before him, so he will be the one to solve the mystery, winning a bride and lands that he does not deserve."

"I have not heard of any mystery here."

"That's because it's no mystery to us."

Bianca opened her mouth to insist that it most definitely was a mystery to her, then closed it again as Hazel leaned in closer.

"Wait and see. Brenna has a plan that will confound even the queen. We are the king's daughters and we will not be held prisoner against our will. Not even Efe and a whole army of beggars will stop us." With another wink, Hazel led the way up the steps to the palace proper, carrying the jug of wine.

Six

Several hours later, when Bianca could barely keep her eyes open, she was startled into alertness by the clatter of metal at her feet. She peered under the table. A sword, still in its scabbard, attached to an unbuckled swordbelt, lay on the flagstones.

A snore cut through the air like a rusty saw, before something clunked to the table beside her. Bianca bumped her head painfully in her haste to see what it was this time. The man at her side had fallen face-first onto the table, and the snoring came from him.

"Finally," Brenna said, rising. The other girls followed her example, and Bianca struggled to her feet.

Bianca swayed, exhaustion conquering her as surely

as it had the unknown man. The unknown, boring man she would sooner die than marry, she knew now.

"I'm going to bed," Bianca mumbled, stumbling in the direction she vaguely remembered led to the bedchamber she'd share with her sisters.

"But you must come dancing with us!" one of the other girls said.

"'Nother night," she managed to say.

"Let her rest," she heard Hazel say as someone took her arm, leading her. "She's been travelling all day. Tomorrow, she can dance."

Dance? Bianca could do many things, but dancing wasn't one of them. Grace was not one of her virtues. She opened her mouth to say so, but all that came out was an unintelligible yawn, followed by another one.

Somehow, she found herself on a soft surface. A bed, she hoped, but she was too tired to care, as sleep enticed her into a dream where dogs drank wine, beggars wore silk and princesses served their every whim as crows cawed from the heavens.

Seven

Waking in a darkened room where the only sound was the even breathing of what Bianca thought must be a dozen sleepers disoriented her at first. She had never shared a sleeping chamber before, and the tiny cubicle that had been hers in the capital had always glowed with the first light of dawn. Groggily, she rolled out of bed, dressed, and padded to the door.

As she reached to push it open, Bianca nearly tripped over something on the floor. She caught herself in time, and shoved the door open to let in enough light to investigate the obstacle. Bianca almost laughed at what appeared to be a pile of worn-out dancing slippers, so hard used the soles bore huge holes. They'd been piled artfully in a drift just inside the door, where anyone trying to enter or exit the room would certainly trip over them and wake everyone.

Bianca surveyed the room, but by some magic, she hadn't woken any of her sisters. Pushing the door open wider, she stepped out of the room, and found the reason for her sisters' makeshift security measures. The adventurer who'd been sleeping on the table last night now lay snoring on a pallet beside the entrance to their room.

Wondering whether he was supposed to be a guard or if he intended to waylay one of the girls when they emerged from their chamber, Bianca did her best to be quiet as she crossed the room and made her way to the dining hall.

The empty table bore no signs of last night's meal, or anything with which to break her fast. Which was strange, given the sun showed it was mid-morning at least. In the women's palace at the capital, the benches would be full of minor wives, concubines and princesses, gossiping like the brightly coloured birds they resembled, as they tried to work out who was missing and hence who the king had favoured to share his bed the previous night. For it was common knowledge in the harem that he and the queen had not shared a bed since she bore his son and heir.

But there would be no such gossip here. The girls all shared a room, and would continue to do so until they died old maids. Unloved, untouched and unwanted. It was no surprise Brenna had brought her little dog along. It was a wonder no one else had pets. If she was forced to live in exile here for the rest of her days, Bianca might consider getting one. A cat, perhaps.

She found her way to the kitchen, where it sounded like the household servants were having their breakfast.

"Anyone willing to place a wager on the latest one?" Bianca heard one girl ask.

A loud snort silenced the rest of them. "That one? Guzzled his wine down like he'd never tasted it before. Probably hadn't. No one will solve the mystery, least of all these adventurers who keep showing up. When it was princes and such, maybe they had a chance, but these men? I wouldn't trust them anywhere near my daughters, and I don't know why the king does."

Someone made hushing sounds. "Don't talk treason. You never know who's listening."

The woman wouldn't be silenced. "It's no treason to speak the truth. I don't know why the king does what he does. But if he's so desperate to see this mystery solved, seems to me he'd only have to question the girls. Not send in some stranger to investigate for him. It sounds like something out of a story, from someone with too much imagination. Next thing you know, there'll be witches and curses and magical gifts, and someone will fall in love."

"You'd better hope none of the princesses falls in love with one of those men. The king would never let one of his daughters marry a nobody."

A clatter told Bianca they were clearing the table.

"But he wouldn't be a nobody any more if he solves the mystery, will he? Even if the man is a beggar, he'd become master of this house."

"Yes, but if they were to fall in love before he solved the mystery…"

Someone laughed. "Then he'd better solve the mystery, or lose his love!"

Dying to ask more about this mystery, but not wishing them to know what she'd overheard, Bianca scuffed her feet deliberately along the flagstones before she entered the kitchen. She found all eyes on her for a stunned moment before they were lowered in respect.

"Your highness," a woman murmured, and the rest chorused something similar.

"I've recently arrived," Bianca began, "so I don't know when or where meals are served here. I fear that I have missed breakfast, yet I am so hungry…"

"I'll fetch you something directly, your highness," a

girl said, bobbing in such a way that Bianca wasn't sure if she was trying to bow or curtsey. Both, maybe. "Where would you like to be served?"

Bianca was stunned into silence for a moment. Never before had she been given a choice in such a thing. A minor princess ate at the common table in the harem, sitting in a spot designated by her rank. For the first time in her life, Bianca was her own mistress. The freedom both frightened and exhilarated her.

"I will eat in the hall where we dined last night," she said breathlessly.

As if reading her thoughts, the girl bobbed again and replied, "As you wish, mistress."

Bianca managed a nod in response before she left the kitchen. Her feet felt strangely light, as though she walked on air. Free. She was free of the miasma of politics she'd lived with so long in the harem. Perhaps she could even…

She returned to the kitchen. "Once I am finished eating, have someone saddle my horse. I wish to ride."

Bianca half expected someone to tell her she couldn't, or caution her against leaving the palace, but the only reply she relieved was a colourless, "Yes, mistress," from one of the people bustling about.

An hour later, when she sat astride the same horse she'd ridden yesterday, Bianca could barely believe it. No one came out to stop her. Why, she could kick the mare into a gallop and leave all this behind forever, if she chose.

For a moment, Bianca was tempted, but she resisted. She knew little of the world outside the walls of the palace. There could be wild animals or anything out there. But Kun had said she was safe inside the palace estate.

Kun. She would ride for Kun's cottage, and visit the old woman. Perhaps even practice a little magic while she was there. After all, she was free to do as she wished now.

Bianca urged the horse into a comfortable pace, feeling a smile light up her face more brightly than the morning sun. Who knew exile would feel so good?

Eight

Vasco's stomach growled, reminding him that it has been many hours since he had eaten his last crust of bread. The incessant hunger pangs were almost enough to make him forget the pain in his knee. In battle, he had scarcely felt the prick of the arrow as it worked its way between his armour, so it was a cruel twist of fate indeed that with every step he took, he had to grit his teeth as pain pierced his knee again and again. Such a small wound had yet made him unfit for war, so his commanding officer had kindly chosen to send him home.

For a married man, or one with any family at all, this would be a blessing. For Vasco, whose entire family had been slaughtered before his village was burned to the ground by the enemy, it was the worst kind of curse. No home, no family, nowhere to go, nothing to do. Vengeance had spurred him to join the army in the first place, but he lost his taste for violence as quickly as it had come. It was too late to protect those he had lost. No matter how many lives he took, he could not bring them back. So he had learned to fight for families and homes that were not his own. If he could save just one village, or someone's parents and brothers and sisters, someone's wife and children, so that no one else had to endure the emptiness inside that ate at him every day, perhaps Vasco would understand why his life had been spared.

Now, understanding eluded him. He had killed, and he had survived, but a single arrow had ended his purpose. So he wandered, doing whatever work he could to earn enough to eat, and sometimes even a place to sleep at night. Or he could, if he saw another soul he could ask for work. These woods he'd wandered into confounded him. The road stretched empty before and behind him, and he had not seen even a single dwelling for two days. If he did not find somewhere soon, he would have to hunt for food. Vasco's lips curled with distaste at the thought of having to use his bow. He was a foot soldier, not an archer, but fate seemed to wish it otherwise.

A hundred steps, he promised himself. He would walk a hundred more steps, and if he did not see any sign of civilisation, he would attempt to make camp and hunt for something for dinner.

Even if it involved… ten, eleven, twelve… archery. He grimaced. He counted forty-seven steps as he rounded a bend, but the forest hugged the road as happily as before. At seventy-nine, climbing a rise in the road, he almost considered changing it to two hundred steps or maybe even three. But the pain in his knee was growing insistent. He needed to stop, and soon. Sighing, Vasco topped the rise. And stopped.

At first, he only saw one house, tucked between the trees. But as his eyes adjusted, he realised he wasn't looking at an isolated cottage in the woods, but enough of them to count as a town. The trees had been thinned to allow space for the houses, but they still towered above them, hiding the place from watchful eyes as they kept their secrets. Though what sort of watchful eye could spy on a village from the very sky itself, Vasco did not know. In fact, he almost laughed at himself for entertaining such a strange notion. Eyes in the sky, indeed! Why, they would have to belong to birds.

Concluding that hunger had scrambled his wits, Vasco resolved to deal with that first. As was his custom when arriving at a new place, he first took stock of the businesses. After all, a thriving business was more likely to have work for him than a humble cottage. He might be lame, jobless and homeless, but Vasco was too proud to beg. As long as he could work to pay for a meal, he was not yet worthless. He squinted at the first shop sign. It showed a garish coloured woman's shoe that no woman he'd ever met could afford. Only a queen or perhaps a princess would wear something in such a bright shade of purple.

But it might tempt a woman who had heard too many fairytales and dreamed of one day being a queen. She might then choose to enter the shop, so that the shoemaker might grant her a smaller dream: that of a new pair of shoes. Perhaps it was not as silly a sign as he'd thought. And a clever shoemaker who could turn a fine profit might have need of a hard worker, and the wherewithal to pay him. This was as good a bet as any.

Vasco pushed open the door and stepped inside. A bell tinkled, announcing his presence before he could open his mouth.

"You are early, sir," a voice said. A man appeared in a doorway behind the counter, his eyes widening when he caught sight of Vasco. "You are not one of the palace servants, unless the king has spent so much money on shoes that he can no longer clothe his servants in proper livery." He laughed as if this was some sort of joke.

Vasco's voice was grave. "I served the king as a faithful soldier, until my superiors said the wounds I had received in battle made me unfit to fight any more." He spread his hands wide. "Now, I ask if you have any work I might do, so that I might earn a meal and perhaps a bed for the night, to help me make my way home." Vasco did not say that he no longer had a home. He had already learned that it was unwise to mention the possibility of staying in a village where he was a stranger. Better to earn a place through hard work and then be invited to stay. His village had been no different. His heart tightened in his chest. At least, it had been. Now, there was no one left but strangers. For all his own people were dead.

The shoemaker squinted at him. "A soldier, eh? Have you any experience in making shoes?"

Vasco shook his head. "I wear shoes, but the making of them is a mystery to me." He managed a faint smile.

The shoemaker sighed. "Then you are out of luck, wounded soldier. I could do with a skilled assistant for I am busier than I ever believed possible. But I have no time to train an apprentice, especially one who has never shown any interest or aptitude for making ladies' shoes."

Vasco bowed his head. "I understand," he said.

"Would you know of any other business in town who might be able to offer me a day's work?" He did not let desperation colour his tone yet. After all, he had gone longer without food before.

The shopkeeper grimaced. "If this were any other town, you would have more luck. But this is Slipper Town, and our trade is shoes for the palace. If you're not a shoemaker, there is no work for you here."

A whole town of shoemakers? Vasco found that hard to believe. In the capital, perhaps, but out here, in the middle of the woods? "Who buys so many shoes?" Vasco demanded.

"The king, of course," the shopkeeper replied cheerfully. "He has many wives, and many daughters. And each must have shoes befitting a lady of the court."

Vasco frowned. "But the court is far from here, surely."

The shopkeeper chuckled. "Ah, but the Summer Palace is very close. And the princesses there need more shoes than the rest of the court put together." He winked, as though they shared a secret.

A secret Vasco did not know, but what cared he for princesses? He was a lowly soldier, who would never be allowed to catch a glimpse of such a high lady. He would happily live and die with no knowledge of such strange creatures. There was but one woman he wished to see again, but as long as he lived, he would only see her in his dreams. She had perished along with the rest of his village.

The shopkeeper's voice broke through his reverie. "Perhaps you should ask at the palace." The shopkeeper coughed. "With so many of the king's precious daughters in residence, the palace is surely in need of more guards."

Vasco thanked him for his advice, and ask for directions to the palace. Vasco was surprised to hear that it was but an hour or two's travel from the village – he could reach the palace by nightfall. Thanking the man once more, Vasco returned to the road.

From the array of signs showing similarly brightly coloured slippers, he realised the truth of the shoemaker's words. This was indeed Slipper Town. A town of shoemakers and little else. The palace must be large indeed, with hundreds of female residents, to keep so many tradesmen in business. Perhaps even large enough to offer him a bed and meals for the rest of his life.

He set off up the road, a new spring in his step for the first time. For deep in his heart, Vasco felt the stirrings of hope.

Nine

Bianca settled into a new routine quickly. She woke with the dawn, while her sisters slept on until well past noon. After breaking her fast, she rode or walked to Kun's cottage. On her return, she would walk beside the lake. Some days it was mirror calm, reflecting the sky and birds above as though there were a second world below, if she but had the courage to pierce the surface. On other days, the beach vanished beneath an onslaught of waves blown up by the slightest breeze, and the lake licked at the very foundations of the Summer Palace.

She grew more skilled at making things invisible. She'd managed to vanish most things in Kun's cottage, before making them visible again. Today, Kun had insisted she bespell the cottage roof. Except she was not to make it vanish entirely – oh, no. Kun asked her to vanish patches of it so that there appeared to be holes in the roof, yet anyone looking through those holes would see nothing of what went on within her house.

The strange twist on her invisibility spell had made Bianca work harder at her magic than ever before. She'd felt worn out by the time she'd accomplished it, only to find Kun demanding proof that the spell had worked. That meant climbing on the cottage roof and peering in.

Bianca had protested at first – after all, princesses did not climb on roofs. Her mother would be horrified at the very thought – but Kun was adamant that one of them must, and the old woman was hardly spry enough to make the climb.

Bianca managed to hoist herself onto the water butt and scramble onto the roof without too much trouble, but climbing down had been her undoing. She'd hit the lid of the water butt on the way down wrong so that it tilted, and instead of landing firmly on it with both feet, she'd slid into the cold water. The butt was easily as deep as she was tall – Bianca might have drowned had Kun not witnessed her fall. As it was, the woman had reached in, seized her collar and dragged the spluttering princess to the surface where she could breathe again.

While Bianca's clothes dried in the sun, she sat in her shift before the fire with a scalding cup of tea in her hands to ward off the chill from her immersion. Kun didn't ask her to perform any more magic, so Bianca decided it was her turn to do the asking today.

"What is this mystery in the palace everyone keeps talking about?" Bianca said, blowing on her tea to cool it.

"Do you mean the shoes?" Kun asked as she poured herself some tea.

The shoes were no mystery, Bianca was sure of it. The other girls piled them up to keep adventurers out of their sleeping chamber, for she'd counted at least half a dozen different men who'd come and gone. They shared the princesses' table and slept on a pallet outside their door for three nights, before they disappeared, never to return.

More than once, Bianca had wondered whether the men were some sort of illusion she'd conjured to keep her hopes alive of finding a husband and a way out of exile, but she knew the men were real. The first adventurer, who'd dropped his sword beneath the table on her first night in the Summer Palace, had neglected to retrieve it. Bianca had found the sword, scabbard and belt several days after his departure, half-hidden under the bench where he'd sat. She'd carried it all to her bedchamber and concealed the items under her bed. The sharp steel was real enough, so the sword's bearer must have been real, too. As were all the adventurers who claimed to be able to solve the mystery. A mystery so mysterious even Bianca didn't know what it was.

"I don't know. The mystery that draws men to the palace like flies to honey," Bianca said finally. "I know men are fools when faced with a beautiful woman – we learned that with our first breath in my father's harem – but they seem taken…nay, obsessed with the notion that they can solve some mystery and claim one of us as a wife. It's not just them, either. The servants say the same. Whoever solves the mystery will become master of the Summer Palace and marry one of us. If I have to make myself invisible to avoid it, I swear his bride will not be me."

She meant it, too, Bianca realised. She would not trade her freedom in exile for marriage to some lusty brute she barely knew.

"The choice may not be up to you," Kun chided. "If the king offers a man a princess for a bride, he might also offer the man his choice of his daughters."

Bianca shuddered. To be given away as a prize, instead of a marriage alliance…as though she were a possession instead of a person…it chilled her. Her father was many things, both bad and good, but he was fiercely protective of his family. "What would make my father offer his own flesh and blood as a prize to any man?"

Kun grinned gummily. "Have you noticed anything unusual about the shoes?"

"They are worn out," Bianca replied. "My sisters pile up their worn-out dancing shoes on the threshold to our sleeping chamber, to trip the unwary adventurer if he seeks to enter without our permission." Permission that would never be granted, she was certain of it.

"So they do, and every morning, a maid comes to tidy away the broken shoes. She throws them on the refuse heap, and brings new shoes for each princess. Yet the next morning, there are more broken shoes." Kun drank deeply from her teacup. "How do you explain this?"

It was on the tip of Bianca's tongue to say that her sisters must have quite a store of broken shoes, or they retrieved them every night from the refuse heap. But that could not be. None of them would soil themselves by setting foot anywhere near the refuse heap, especially not to claim some old shoes. Instead, she said, "I can't."

"And nor can the king, or any of the adventurers who hear of this mystery. That is why the king has offered the Summer Palace and the hand of a princess in marriage to any man who can solve the mystery for him." Kun set her empty cup on the table.

Bianca still didn't understand. "All that because of some shoes?"

Kun shook her head slowly. "Not just some shoes. A dozen pairs of dancing shoes every night. Fine shoes suitable for a princess. Why, it would take a dozen craftsmen more than a day to make such shoes. And all the silk and leather that must be used to make them…why, you and your sisters will bankrupt the treasury if this keeps on much longer. What else can your father do but offer a reward to anyone who can find him a solution before you and your sisters run his treasury dry?"

"I have not had a single pair of new shoes since I arrived," Bianca objected. "Nor have I worn any out. My father cannot blame me for whatever it is my sisters do. I will not be punished for their carelessness!" She rose and stormed outside to where her clothes were almost dry. She dressed quickly, ignoring the way the still-damp cloth clung to her. It would surely dry on the ride home.

With a curt farewell to Kun, Bianca spurred her horse toward the Summer Palace.

"Not all women see marriage as a punishment," Kun called softly after her. "If you marry a good man, what feels like duty at first can be a pleasure, in time."

The horse snorted, echoing Bianca's sentiments. She might have lived a sheltered life, but she'd lived in a harem. A harem full of wives who spoke little of the pleasures of marriage. If a woman wanted pleasure of any kind, she must make it for herself. The pleasure of a refreshing ride, or a brisk walk by the lake. Such were the pleasures available to her now, and Bianca found very little enjoyment in Kun's company if the old woman intended to harp on about duty.

Instead, she would ask her sisters to let her know their secret, and protect it so fiercely no man would pry it from her. For if no man solved the mystery, no man could marry one of them. It was the perfect solution.

Ten

After an hour's journey up the road, with no signs of the palace or even a break in the woods, Vasco was ready to curse the shoemaker into oblivion for his poor directions. But, he reasoned, his steps were slower than most, what with his limp and all, so perhaps the shoemaker's directions were for a fitter man than he. Or the palace was as well hidden as the village. Neither would have surprised him, so he trudged wearily on.

This time, when he saw a cottage, he paused to scan the woods for the rest of the village. However, this cottage truly did stand alone. From its falling down state, he doubted anyone lived there now. But an empty cottage that no one lived in was a place he could happily spend the night. Nevertheless, the door to this cottage stood shut, so he knocked tentatively on it instead of barging inside.

To his surprise, a querulous elderly voice said, "Who is it?"

Vasco wet his lips, suddenly nervous. "My name is Vasco," he said. "I am a wounded soldier, recently returned from war. I seek a meal, and perhaps a bed for the night, and, in exchange, I offer my services." He eyed the holes in the roof. "For instance, I could fix your roof so that the next time it rains, it no longer leaks."

The door creaked open and a wrinkled face peered out. "Fixing my roof is no small job," she said. "You would need a place to sleep for more than one night, and you'd more than earn your meals between."

Vasco smiled at the old woman. "Honoured grandmother, we have a deal."

She eyed him suspiciously. "I'm not your grandmother, boy. I'd remember a strapping soldier like you. You can call me Kun." She gave him another hard look before she added, "And you can sleep in the barn with the goats." She cackled. "For I've no use for a handsome soldier in my bed. Not at my age."

Vasco smiled wistfully, for now, she reminded him of his own grandmother. She had not lived to see her village slaughtered. "You must have few visitors, if you think me handsome. And I have better luck with goats than women, so the barn is a good place for me." After all, three goats had survived the massacre of his village. Three goats and one man, but no women. Goats' milk had kept him alive long enough to join the army, when he traded them for the price of his weapons and armour. None of them had been his family's goats, but he had reasoned that the spirits of the slain would have happily handed over their last livestock in order to exact vengeance from their murderers. Perhaps it would help their spirits rest. For Vasco knew it would be a long time before he would know a good night's rest.

"Come in, then," Kun said, stepping back and holding the door wide open. "There is soup in the pot, and fresh straw in the barn. It will be dark soon, and repairs can wait until morning."

Gratefully, Vasco stepped into the dark cottage, his stomach rumbling so loudly at the first whiff of soup that he hardly heard the door slam shut behind him.

Eleven

It was not to be, Bianca found when she reached home. Her sisters were already in the dining hall, studiously ignoring a new adventurer whose eye-watering pink robe fit so badly Bianca wondered whether Efe was trying to blind them.

The new man was well into his cups when his eyes fixed on her. "Well, aren't you a pretty one?" he slurred. "Mayhap I'll take you to wife, so I can see if you're as pale under that robe as you are above it."

Bianca was too tired to be courteous to this buffoon. "I assure you, I am not. Beneath this robe, I'm covered in thick fur like one of the bears from the mountains. I must shave my face every morning to stop the fur from growing. And cut my claws, lest I disembowel someone by mistake." She curled her fingers into claws and bared her teeth.

Hazel choked on her soup. Aruna had to pound her on the back as a coughing fit engulfed her, effectively ending the conversation for several minutes.

When she thought no one was looking, Brenna set her dog on the table, who scampered straight for the man's goblet. Bianca had to smother a laugh, for this wasn't the first time she'd seen Brenna set the dog on their unwanted dinner guests. She was certain her sister had trained the animal to only drink from a man's cup. Or perhaps he only drank wine, for all her sisters' cups contained water tonight.

"Cursed creature!" With a backhand blow, he sent the little, yelping dog flying off the table to hit the wall. It slid to the floor, looking stunned, before it crawled under the table to hide from the horrible man.

"I shall fetch you some fresh wine," Bianca said through gritted teeth, wishing she could slip poison into the cup. No man who hurt a helpless animal so deserved to live, let alone marry. What if he treated his wife that way?

She swept out of the room before he could say anything more. Bianca considered heading to her bedchamber for the sword beneath her bed, but she dismissed the idea almost as soon as she'd thought of it. She'd never handled a sword, and with his greater strength, he would easily beat her in a fight. Women didn't wield swords, anyway. They fetched wine and waited for the fool to fall asleep.

The jug she carried back was so full a little slopped over the brim at every step, but grim determination drove her. Bianca would do her best to get the man to drink himself to death before he could do the dog further injury.

She filled his cup, and filled it again, until the jug was empty. To her chagrin, he seemed no closer to succumbing to sleep than he had earlier. Yet her own eyes felt heavy, what with all the climbing and spell-casting she'd done at Kun's today.

Bianca rose unsteadily to her feet. "More wine," she muttered, stumbling a little as she headed for the door.

Hazel appeared at her elbow. "Let me help you, sister," she said, prying the jug from Bianca's fingers.

Bianca gratefully accepted the other girl's arm. "I went for a long ride today. Too long, I think. So….tired," she yawned.

Hazel glanced back at the dining hall. "His boasting is enough to put anyone to sleep. Retire early. I'll fetch the wine and make your excuses." She gave Bianca a push in the direction of their sleeping chamber.

Bianca nodded and did as she was bidden. It wasn't until she was tucked in her bed that she remembered wanting to ask her sisters about the mystery. Ah, it would wait until morning. It wasn't like the mystery was going anywhere. They'd want a huge pile of shoes to guard against tonight's buffoon.

She drifted off into dreamless sleep.

Twelve

As Vasco slid from the roof, he tried to think of a way to tell Kun that she was lucky her house hadn't fallen down around her ears. Yet. But he was a soldier, not a diplomat.

"Well?" Kun demanded, her hands on her hips.

Vasco blew out a breath. "You were right," he said heavily. "The roof doesn't need repairing as much as it needs replacing completely. I think some of the beams are rotten, too. I noticed last night that one of the barn walls has a definite lean to it, though the roof is in better repair. If it rains, my bed with the goats might be drier than yours here in the house."

Her eyes were shrewd as she regarded him. "So

how long do you propose to squash my straw and eat my larder bare, soldier boy?"

Vasco looked her in the eye. "As long as you have work you wish me to do, ma'am." He coughed. "But the repairs to your roof and the barn will likely take a week or two, depending on how long it takes me to find good timber."

Kun waved at the woods around. "There are trees aplenty, boy. Take your pick."

He nodded. "A week, then."

"A week's work for just room and board? Surely you will ask for more than that," she said.

Vasco spread his arms wide. "It is all I ask," he said carefully. "But if you choose to gift me with something more, I will not refuse."

She nodded slowly. "Very well. A bed, board, and a gift to match how good a job you do. We have a deal, though you are a fool to accept it."

He shrugged. "We are all foolish at some point in our lives. But no more foolish than necessary. Which is why I think I shall spend the morning chopping firewood for you before I take your axe into the woods, for a hard worker deserves a hot meal at the end of the day. That soup you made last night was the best I've ever tasted."

"Flatterer," Kun scoffed. "I'll wager your mother makes better."

"Alas, my mother roams the spirit world now. She has no need for soup, not that she ever did. My father hated the stuff, so she never made it." Vasco bowed his head briefly before turning away and making his way toward the chopping block. If his eyes seemed watery, and he had to blink back what felt suspiciously like tears, no one would see.

He swung the axe a little harder than necessary, but he told himself that Kun needed kindling as much as big logs to burn the night through. He could no longer cut down his enemies, but a few trees would fall to his frustration before the day was out.

The skin of his back crawled, as if someone was watching him, but Vasco ignored it. It was probably only Kun, not some enemy who would attack him. Right now his only enemy was wood, and he was more than a match for it.

Thirteen

When day dawned, Bianca stepped over the pile of shoes without a second thought. She tiptoed past the snoring adventurer and made her way to the dining hall, where she knew breakfast would be served for her. While she ate, the kitchen staff prepared a basket of provisions for her to take on her ride. Usually she gave most of it to Kun in thanks for the woman's time training her, for there was far too much for one person, but Bianca wondered what the staff would say if she returned with a basket that wasn't empty.

They might send less food with her on the morrow, she decided, which would not do. She had no other way of repaying Kun.

So, though it was the last place she wanted to go after Kun's comments yesterday, she guided her horse along the road to the old woman's house.

The sound of an axe biting into wood stopped her before she reached the cottage. Tethering her horse to a tree, out of sight of the road, Bianca paused for only a moment to render herself invisible before she continued on foot.

It was probably some villager, looking for some healing herbs or a good luck charm from Kun. It wasn't the first time Bianca had arrived when Kun had a customer, so she was content to wait until the man was gone. A princess shouldn't speak to the villagers, especially not the men. For the adventurers Efe set at their table were coarse enough, under the thin veneer of good manners they assumed, but a peasant who had no need to pretend to be polite might do anything.

Bianca's invisibility might protect her somewhat, but it did nothing to hide the sound she made. Or her scent, if the man had a dog. And if he were to bump into her…but he wouldn't get close enough for that, Bianca resolved as she crept closer.

She skirted Kun's cottage, heading to the yard where she knew the chopping block stood.

The man wielding the axe was no villager, though. Unless he was the blacksmith. She'd never seen so much muscle on a man, and there was plenty to see, for he was naked to the waist, with sweat gleaming on his broad chest. A scarred chest, she noted. If he wasn't a smith, then he had fought battles against men instead of metal. Or some horrible accident had befallen him.

The way he hammered the axe into the hapless chunks of wood spoke of some personal grudge he held against the tree. A section of trunk turned to kindling under his relentless strokes. He swept the spars up in his arms, stacked them in the woodshed, then grabbed another log to dismember. Whoever he was, he showed no sign of slowing. He must have asked for a really complicated spell from Kun, to do so much work in payment.

Bianca settled on the grass to wait.

Hours passed, but he did not slow. If anything, the furrows in his forehead only deepened as he continued to work. He allowed the timber to break into bigger pieces than kindling now before he stacked them in the woodshed, too.

He circled the chopping block, giving Bianca a clear view of his equally well-muscled back. He had fewer scars here, though they weren't entirely absent. What did that mean? That when he fought, he faced his enemy head on, and never turned his back on them?

Bianca felt the most peculiar urge to ask him. She could return to the road, dismiss her invisibility spell, and stroll into the yard as though she'd just arrived. She could offer him some of her provisions and introduce herself as Bianca. Not a princess, just…a maid from the palace. There. That would do. She rose to her feet, determined to put her plan into action.

"You've been working hard. You must be hungry. Come inside. The noon meal is ready," Kun said.

The woodcutter swiped his arm across his face, then grabbed a tunic he'd hung on the edge of the woodshed roof and pulled the garment over his head, hiding those delicious muscles from sight.

Delicious? Bianca scoffed at herself for having such thoughts. Why would she want to lick the man's sweaty skin? It would be hard and salty and…definitely unpleasant, she told herself. She was just hungry, that was all.

She rose, stretching the cramps from her legs from sitting so long, before heading back to the road in search of her horse. The mare stood exactly where she'd been left, with no sign of distress at being invisible. Bianca could see her, of course, as she could with anything she bespelled, but if she concentrated, she could also see what everyone else saw – nothing.

She grabbed the first thing she touched in the basket and bit into it. The sweetness told her it was fruit, but that's all the attention she paid to food. Her thoughts were with the scarred man in Kun's cottage.

Who was he?

Fourteen

With every limping step, Vasco reminded himself how much he hated archery. This hadn't always been the case, of course, for archery practice had been a required part of his training. He'd even been good at it once. Now, though…he hadn't been able to bring himself to fire an arrow at the enemy since he'd been wounded. Shooting someone from a distance was cowardly, especially if you couldn't give them a clean death. If they fell before you and you had a sword or an axe, it was a simple matter to deliver another blow if the first hadn't killed them. With arrows, though, it was much harder to hit someone who'd fallen. And no man, friend or foe, deserved to live with the constant pain he did. Wounds either healed or they killed you. They weren't supposed to torment you for the rest of your life.

Yet he nailed the slice of tree trunk to a tree on the edge of Kun's yard, and it became an archery target. Because while he might never shoot another man, he would undoubtedly need to hunt for his dinner one day. If he could not shoot something for the pot, then he would go hungry.

Besides, archery practice had always been his favourite part of army training. His thoughts grew clear and singular, focussed only on the target and the conditions that might affect his shot.

As if carried by a breeze from the distant past, he thought he heard the bark of some long-dead training officer shouting the drill: Stance. Nock. Draw. Aim. Loose. All followed by a bellowed, "AGAIN!"

Vasco marched to the other end of the yard in the pre-dawn light, and began to string his bow. He would shoot until he lost or broke all his arrows, or until Kun woke and he could start work on her cottage for the day.

Stance. He positioned one foot, then the other, ready to move and fire in any direction.

Nock. He'd seen men argue over the best way to do this, which side of the bow and whether to rest the arrow on one's knuckles or one's thumb. Vasco had never bothered to argue. His father had been a good archer, though he never shot an arrow in anger. And he had taught his son the only good way to do it. Vasco's arrows shot from the right side of the bow, over his thumb. He reached for the one of the arrows in the earth at his feet, and nocked it.

There was no wind in the clearing where Kun's cottage lay. Not for the first time, he wondered whether it was luck or if she was a witch. Neither would surprise him. If she was a witch, though, all the more reason not to wake her before she chose to rise.

Draw. Vasco sucked in a breath, held it, and drew the arrow back a little. The bowstring pulled as smoothly as a song.

He sighted along the arrow, aiming for the target, as he drew the arrow back further.

Breathe, he told himself. There was nothing else in the clearing but him, his bow and arrow, the target he intended to hit and the air separating him and his goal. Air he had to breathe.

One…two…three. Vasco loosed his arrow at the target.

It hit, but barely. He had aimed too low.

AGAIN.

Vasco reached for another arrow. It sped off into the trees, missing the target completely.

Vasco swore under his breath.

AGAIN.

By the time Kun called him for breakfast, he had run through his store of arrows three times, but on the third round, he'd managed to hit the target on every shot. Tomorrow, he would do better, he promised himself. If he did not, better to give Kun the bow for firewood than carry it around any longer.

His father's bow was the only thing he'd salvaged from his burned home. That and the goats, of course. His father had kept the weapon in the woodshed, the only building in the village that hadn't burned. Perhaps because it was full of green wood, not yet dry enough to burn, that Vasco and his father had cut the week before the attack.

To burn it would be to lose the last link to home. To his family. To Dokia. Though they all walked with the ancestors now, he would carry their memories with him every day. And his father's bow.

"If you don't come in now, I shall give it to the goats!" Kun threatened.

A very real threat, Vasco knew. He'd let the goats out of the barn to munch on the fresh spring grass for breakfast, but they wouldn't turn their noses up at human food.

He hurried to obey her summons. Tomorrow, he swore. Though to who, he wasn't sure.

Fifteen

After waiting most of the afternoon, during which the muscled man still didn't leave, Bianca reluctantly climbed back on her horse and headed home. It wasn't until she reached the palace that she realised she hadn't given Kun any of the food. Tomorrow, she promised herself, for the man would have gone home by then, surely.

Yet when she returned on the morrow, he was still there, cutting trees and dragging them back to the cottage. He looked bigger and brawnier than she remembered, which only made her feel worse about forgetting to give Kun her basket the previous day. So today she watched and waited, telling herself she was looking for an opportunity to sneak into the cottage unseen so she could repay Kun for her kindness.

Once again, the man did not leave the yard for long enough. He had enough timber to keep him occupied well into the afternoon, when Bianca had to return home.

Every day for a week she returned, and every day she found him still there. She wanted to resent him for keeping her from meeting Kun, but she couldn't. He took such care in his work, cutting the timber so precisely before using it to build Kun a completely new barn. Only when it was finished did she see him smile, and what a change it was. The brooding man seemed to light up from the inside. He took pride in a job well done. Something she had rarely seen in her father's palace, where servants held their positions for life and had no need to be good at their jobs to keep them.

Oh, she'd seen musicians dedicated to their craft, and cooks who cared about what their kitchen created, though the staff under them might not be quite as enthusiastic about such exacting standards, but this? The way this man built that tiny structure to house Kun's goats made her wonder how the architects and builders of the palace in the capital had felt when they regarded their handiwork.

She would never know, for the palace was

completed before she was born, and definitely before she discovered she could use her invisible talents to escape the harem and roam about the palace. She fancied that she was the only princess who had ever entered the kitchens, and watched the soldiers at training in the guardhouse yard, when neither was deemed a fitting place for the king's daughters.

She could have watched the scribes and calligraphers for hours, though, for their painstaking work was akin to art. Only the knowledge that her mother would miss her and know she had escaped sent her back. Otherwise…Bianca fancied she might have joined them. If she had not been born a princess, she would have liked to choose the life of a scribe. Locking up words and whole stories in a series of symbols, so that people miles away or a hundred years into the future could see them and know what had happened. It was a kind of immortality, she supposed.

Now if she could immortalise Kun's carpenter in art, capturing the bulge of his muscles as he hefted the axe, or lifted a new beam into place, or that look of calm concentration he wore when he practiced archery in the early mornings. She'd only caught him at it once, but his makeshift target, a round slice of tree trunk, bore the signs of increasing accuracy as the week progressed.

She imagined him returning home to his lovely,

loving wife – for a man like this could not go unloved – carrying fresh meat he'd caught on the point of his arrow on the way home after finishing work on Kun's cottage. His own cottage would be immaculate inside and out, for a man who took such care on Kun's house would lavish even more attention on the home of the woman he loved.

And at night, beneath that perfectly crafted roof, he would use those skilled hands on his wife, in all the ways they'd whispered about in the harem. Bianca sighed at the thought. She envied the man's wife, for she knew a joy Bianca herself would never know.

Movement sighted out of the corner of her eye roused Bianca from her daydream, and she sat up to find Kun's eyes on her. The old woman beckoned her over, as if she could see the invisible princess as clearly as anything else in her garden.

Bianca glanced around, not seeing the man, so she dismissed the spell and hurried into the house.

"You've been so busy watching Vasco that you've forgotten about me," Kun remarked as she set some water boiling for tea.

Bianca opened her mouth to protest, but the old woman's sharp look silenced her. Instead, she said, "How did you know?"

"I recognise the smell of your magic now, having seen you cast it so often. There is more to this world than what the eyes can see," Kun said. "Though you've been using your eyes more of late, I see."

"What sort of spell did he ask for, to repay you with a beautiful new barn?" Bianca asked. "It must be something difficult. Healing for his wife, perhaps?" The man she'd watched all week would do anything to make his wife well, if she fell ill, Bianca was certain of it.

Kun laughed. "Not all want a spell. And not all men have wives. This one shares a bed with my nanny goats every night, which might be why he built me such a stout barn. He is a soldier, injured in battle, who now wanders while he looks for work. He had thoughts to apply at the Summer Palace."

Bianca's hopes, which had soared at the thought that the man had no wife yet, plummeted to earth at the realisation that he was another adventurer. "So he will appear at our table next, swathed in ill-fitting silk, as he tries to wheedle secrets out of my sisters?"

"He had thoughts to work as a guard, but I have kept him busy here. He's not like the others. The others barely had two words for me before they hustled themselves up to the palace. Vasco is a good man who has no wish for fame and wealth. Not like the others, who would thrust a blade through my body without a second thought if the reward asked for my heart and not the palace secret."

Bianca wet her lips. "So he does not want a bride or a palace?"

Kun's forehead furrowed, then smoothed. "He is a man who keeps his feet solidly on the ground, who might look at the stars above, but will never reach for them. A man who happily shares a barn with goats knows a palace and a princess are far beyond his reach."

"What if he had help?" The words left Bianca's lips before she'd really thought them through.

Kun eyed her suspiciously. "Are you offering to help a man you do not know, and betray your sisters in the same breath?"

Bianca gaped. She, a traitor? Never. "I meant…if you mentioned the king's offer, and told Vasco what you know of the mystery so that he might have a better chance than his predecessors, and maybe encouraged him to try…"

"Do you know what happens to the men who fail to solve the mystery?" Kun demanded.

"They have three days. If they fail, they leave," Bianca said.

"Have you ever seen them leave?"

Bianca shook her head. "No, but they must. They are no longer at the palace."

"Are they?" Kun's eyes were sharp. "There are many cellars beneath the Summer Palace, much like its grander cousin in the capital. It would be easy to turn one into a dungeon to imprison them."

"But why? What would Efe have to gain in imprisoning such men? I don't know how you could imagine such nonsense." Even as she said the words, Bianca didn't believe them. For under her bed, she still had the first adventurer's sword. No man would leave without his sword, the means to defend himself. Yet...why would anyone imprison the man? He had committed no crime. But the sword...

Kun's look was knowing. "Ah, you suspect there is more than nonsense in it. I see it in your eyes. Why should I throw a good man to the wolves? It seems to me he can do a lot more good in his life than try to solve some mystery not even the king knows the answer to. Have you solved it yet?"

Bianca forced herself to admit that she had not. Vasco – if that was indeed the man's name – had distracted her from asking her sisters about it. But if she asked them... "I could help him," she offered eagerly before adding, "Not to betray my sisters. But to stop the flow of beggars and braggarts Efe sends to our table. It is not right. He dresses them like noblemen, but beneath the veneer, I fear that they have few principles. It is only a matter of time before one of them threatens us with violence, or invades our sleeping chamber at night, or..." Bianca shuddered.

She didn't want to think of anything worse, but the images crept to her mind, unbidden. She had heard stories of the things men did to unprotected women. There was a reason she hadn't left the palace grounds alone.

"If you help him, the man may stand a chance," Kun admitted. "But you will rob me of my servant, before he has fashioned a complete new cottage and furnishings for me. A project he seems to enjoy. It will take all my powers of persuasion to make him believe he wants to leave my employ for the uncertainty of a job at the palace. It will cost you more than a basket of food this time, princess."

Bianca recognised the steely look in Kun's eyes. That very same look had made her climb on the cottage roof to see her own handiwork. "Very well," she said. "What would you ask of me in payment for such a service?"

Kun shook her head. "You would not last a day in a village marketplace, let alone the wide world, girl. You should offer a very low price, not let me name mine. That isn't how bargaining is done."

Bianca's lips lifted in a smile she did not feel. "I cut my teeth on politics. The bargaining at court is very different to a common marketplace. Both parties ask for all that they desire, before negotiations commence to whittle down the lists to some sort of compromise where neither are happy, but each gets some of what they wish for. Name your price, and then we shall bargain in earnest."

Kun's eyes widened. Perhaps she had underestimated Bianca, the girl mused. She wagered the witch did not make that mistake often. "A new cloak that is so beautiful, so stunning that no man can look at its wearer and truly see them, but nothing is hidden to the wearer."

Bianca nodded slowly. "You wish me to make you a cloak which will render you invisible, yet able to see the invisible, like I do."

"You're quick, girl."

"Would you like a cloak made of silk, wool, or something else?" Bianca asked.

Kun looked thoughtful. "Silk seems a little too grand. And besides, I already have the cloak. It is your magic I want." Her gnarled finger pointed at the hooks behind the door. Beside her own faded, worn cloak in earthy brown hung another one, much longer and thicker than the first. Dark as a raven's wing, the blackness of it seemed to steal some of the room's light.

It almost seemed alive, for it certainly held its own magic. If Bianca bespelled it so that it made the wearer invisible, it would be a valuable thing indeed.

"We have a bargain," Bianca announced. "I will cast

an invisibility spell on that cloak that also works on its owner, and you shall send your servant to the palace to solve my mystery."

Kun eyed her. "Most would hesitate before making a bargain with a witch, girl. Are you sure?"

Bianca almost laughed. "But we are both witches, and you are the one asking me for a spell, in exchange for a trivial favour. Shouldn't I be asking you if you are sure?"

Kun seemed to consider for a moment, before she nodded. "We have a bargain. Cast your spell, and the man will be at the Summer Palace on the morrow."

The spell was surprisingly simple, shimmering across the cloth like so many stars. Yet when Kun donned the cloak, it hid her completely.

"That will do," Kun said, appearing again as she shrugged off the cloak, which was so long it pooled in the floor around her.

Outside, the rhythmic blows of an axe biting into wood pierced the stillness.

"Good to hear him hard at work," Kun said, jerking her chin in the direction of the yard.

"Tomorrow. You promised," Bianca said, feeling her heart beating fast. It must be the surprise at hearing axe blows, she told herself. Not the prospect of sharing the Summer Palace with Vasco. Why, she barely knew the man.

"I will hold up my end of the bargain. Ancestors help him if you don't keep up yours, though. He will need all the help he can get," Kun replied.

"I'm sure he'll succeed where the others failed," Bianca said, trying to sound more confident than she felt. He had to. Summoning a satisfied smile, she strode out of the cottage, covered her fair skin from the sun, and rode home.

That night, she could scarcely sleep from excitement. But finally she did, only to dream of ravens wheeling in a sky of invisible stars.

Sixteen

This time when Vasco climbed down from the roof, he felt the weariness of the long day's work. But a good day's work. A good week's work, truth be told. He had repaired walls, replaced beams, and Kun's cottage now had a completely new roof. She also had a year's worth of firewood – the remains of the trees Vasco had cut down which had been suitable for nothing but burning. And yes, he'd chop that into suitable lengths for her, too.

He hadn't quite shaken that prickly feeling of being watched, but he'd learned to ignore it. Kun spent most of her time in her cottage, not outside it watching him, and as he'd seen no one else, he concluded that his watchers must be birds. For what novelty could there be in a man rebuilding a house, except for the woman who lived there?

He paused to wash his face in the water butt, and only then did he hear voices. He listened hard, for more than once he had heard Kun talking to herself. No, this was definitely two voices and only one of them was Kun's. The visitor must have arrived while he'd been working on the roof, too busy to notice her arrival.

Not wishing to disturb Kun and her visitor, he peeped through the window. Kun sat at the table, pouring tea, but the visitor had her back to the window. In the dimly lit cottage, all he could see of the visitor was her white hair, carefully braided into one long queue that hung down her back, contrasting with her dark cloak.

Another old woman, he concluded. He debated whether to go and introduce himself, in the hope that Kun's friend might have more work to keep him busy for another week or two. For Kun could not complain about his diligence or even his appetite. Vasco was a hard worker and he knew it. Perhaps it would be better to demonstrate that to the guest, rather than going into the cottage and interrupting their conversation. He headed to the chopping block, where there were still some logs uncut. He had planned to leave them for the morrow, but he was not so tired that he could not cut them now. Levering the axe out of the chopping block where he'd left it that morning, he set to work.

Vasco soon fell into a rhythm, turning one log into suitable pieces for an old woman to carry, before chipping a pile of kindling. He piled his handiwork up in the woodshed before starting on the next.

When the door opened and Kun's visitor emerged, Vasco almost dropped his axe in surprise. In the bright sunlight, her hair appeared a pale gold, not white at all. She moved like a much younger woman then Kun, with her straight back and a pert toss of her head as she stepped out fully.

When Vasco saw her face, the axe fell from his nerveless fingers. This time, he didn't notice. He had eyes only for the fair maiden before him. He had never seen a girl with such fair skin, paler even than her hair. Pink lips and bright eyes, separated by a small, pointed nose, and all lit up with a satisfied smile. A smile that would haunt his dreams for the rest of his life, he was certain. He had only a moment more to stare at the vision before him, before she pulled her hood up, and her face vanished from sight in the depths of her cloak. She mounted a horse Vasco had not seen until now, waved a pale hand at Kun, before urging her mount into a trot.

The moment she disappeared through the trees,

Vasco felt the most powerful sense of loss. It was almost like losing his village all over again.

"Put your eyes back in your sockets, boy," Kun snapped. "You look like a fool who has never seen a pretty girl before."

Vasco found his voice. "I have seen pretty girls before," he said slowly. "But never a creature as beautiful as her." He swallowed. "Who is she?"

Kun cackled. "That is Princess Bianca." She paused as if to let her statement sink in before she continued, "She is one of the king's daughters who lives at the Summer Palace. She is kind enough to come and visit an old lady, and bring me supplies from the palace kitchens." She eyed him speculatively. "But the princess has not come to visit me since you arrived, perhaps scared away by the hulking brute of a soldier. A pity, for you have not tasted palace food. As it is, I was running low on well-nigh everything until she arrived."

Vasco hung his head. "If I have outstayed my welcome, then I shall depart. Your house is repaired, as promised, and I hope I have earned my board and lodging. If you know of anywhere else I might be of service —"

Kun waved him into silence. "Don't be silly, boy. If you had eaten every crumb in my larder, it would be a good bargain for the new house and barn you have built for me. And I might be able to suggest further employment for you, especially if you are interested in seeing the princess again."

Vasco was afraid to meet her eyes. "I would dearly love to see such beauty again, but I fear she is too high for me. Just a glimpse will leave me distracted from my work all day." He cleared his throat. "I had thought to ask at the palace whether they have need of more guards, but now I am certain of it. A palace that keeps such treasures as that princess within its walls can never have enough guards."

Kun smiled faintly. "I don't know about guards, but I do know of one problem the king has with keeping so many princesses in the palace. He has a mystery he wants solved. And any man who can solve this for him will be richly rewarded."

"Will the king provide a lowly soldier with a bed and a meal while he solves this mystery?" Vasco asked.

Kun laughed. "I believe so."

"Then what can you tell me about this mystery?" Vasco asked.

Kun raised her eyebrows. "You ask about the mystery and not the reward? You are a strange man."

Vasco shrugged. "There is no reward unless I can solve the mystery. And if I have a place to eat and sleep, I have little else to worry about."

"Then come inside, for royal mysteries are best

discussed over tea and cakes from the palace kitchens."
Kun beckoned him inside, and Vasco followed.

Seventeen

Bianca paced along the lakeshore while she waited impatiently for her sisters to wake or for Vasco to arrive. She hadn't cared about any of the previous adventurers, but she wanted to speak to him. To see if he truly was different from the others, like Kun had said.

The sun had already started to sink by the time a maid finally came to tell her that her sisters were awake.

Bianca thanked the girl, then added, "Do you know if any visitors have arrived?"

The girl frowned and shook her head. "No, mistress."

Surely Kun wouldn't have broken her bargain, would she? They had a deal. A bargain between two witches wasn't to be broken lightly, Bianca knew. But the day wasn't over yet. Perhaps Kun had kept Vasco for one more day to finish working on her roof, and he needed daylight to work. It might be dark by the time her arrived at the palace, if there was a lot of work to do.

In the meantime, she would find out all she could from her sisters, Bianca decided. She headed inside, and found her sisters seated in the dining hall, breaking their fast, though it was well into the afternoon.

Bianca slid into an empty spot on the bench. "Good day," she began.

A chorus of mumbled responses came back to her.

Bianca hid a smile. They really had just awoken. "I've been wondering for a while now, and I must ask. Why the pile of shoes at the door every morning? I have lost count of the number of times I have tripped over them."

A few of the girls shared smiles, and Brenna laughed. She set her dog down on the floor with a bowl of food she'd selected from the table for the animal. "You mean the shoes we have all danced to pieces?"

Bianca nodded. "They do look quite worn. I wonder why you would keep shoes in such a state."

Hazel laughed. "We don't keep them. We pile them up so that the servants can throw them on the refuse heap, and Cousin Efe will have new shoes made to replace them. He's been sending up new shoes for you, though you haven't danced at all since you arrived."

"I don't dance," Bianca said, ducking her head. She reached for a piece of bread.

"But you must," Aruna exclaimed. "Tonight, you will come with us. I promise you, you will feel like the most graceful dancer in the world once you have the right partner."

A vision of Vasco popped into Bianca's head, and she blushed. "The right partner?" she echoed, trying to rid her mind of the thought of Vasco holding her in his arms.

"Oh, yes," Nera gushed. "Just wait until you see – "

A masculine cough interrupted her. All the girls fell silent.

Efe stepped into the room with a simpering smile on his face. "My dear princesses, may I present Lord Vasco?"

Lord Vasco? Bianca choked.

Eighteen

Princesses who danced their shoes to pieces? And a king who was so insistent upon knowing why that he would hire a man just to solve the mystery of the worn shoes?

Even as Vasco trudged up the road to the palace, away from the comfort of Kun's cottage, he shook his head in disbelief. He had seen the town of shoemakers, so he knew there was some truth in these princesses who wore out shoes faster than a soldier wore out boots, but there had to be more to this mystery than first appeared.

Why else would Kun have given him so much advice? She'd told him to refuse any food or wine that the princesses themselves did not consume. If he wanted to know what the girls did at night, he must enter their bedchamber before the door was locked — as though he dared enter a princess's bedchamber! Yet she'd told him to hide there, and wear the new cloak she'd given him, as though the black wool would conceal him completely in what would surely be a well-lit chamber. And to top it all off, she'd said he only had three days in which to solve the mystery, so if he ran into difficulties, he was to approach Princess Bianca, the pale beauty he'd espied at Kun's cottage, and ask her for help. As if such a highborn princess would stoop to assist someone as worthless as him.

But Kun had insisted, and he had repeated all of her advice, until she was satisfied that he remembered it all. Still, he didn't trust what he'd heard, so instead of approaching the front entrance as Kun had told him to, Vasco skirted the building until he found the servants' entrance, and knocked there, instead.

The maid who answered the door wore a dress far finer than anything the women in Vasco's village had ever owned. For a moment, his voice died in his throat as he wondered if he'd somehow arrived at a private entrance to the princesses' quarters instead.

Vasco's hands tightened around the hat he held level with his belt. "I came seeking work, and an old woman down the road told me the master of this house might have need of a man."

The girl's eyes held sympathy as she shook her head. "There is no position here that I know of. We are but a small household. I don't know why Mistress Kun would send you here. She of all people knows…" She swallowed. "Unless she sent you here to solve the mystery?"

Vasco gave a nod. "She did mention a mystery."

"Are you sure?" the girl asked. "You will only have three days, and no one else has managed to solve it in that time. You aren't like the others…"

The others being princes and lords, noblemen who were accustomed to being in the presence of princesses, Vasco assumed. Not common soldiers like him. Yet Kun had been confident he could do this thing.

"I must try," he said finally. "I have nothing else. No home, no family, and nothing to occupy me once the army had finished with me. Unless you can point me to somewhere else where I might find work, this is the only employment for miles around."

Now she looked almost pitying. "I understand. What is your name, soldier?"

"Vasco," he answered.

"I'm Gerel," she said. "I will tell the Lord Steward you are here. If there is no other suitor, he will introduce you to the princesses and you will be in their company for three days until you solve the mystery or are banished from this place. But…if you wish for company, or more plain fare than is served in the dining hall, or if the Lord Steward will not see you, I pray you will come to the kitchen. There will be a place for you at our table, for anyone who can tell us about what goes on outside the estate is welcome. We are very isolated here."

As isolated as his own village before it was wiped out, Vasco thought, though he couldn't bring himself to say the words aloud. Not to this pretty maid who had probably never seen any sort of violence in her life, much like the princesses she served. Gerel deserved to marry one of the manservants of the house and live in the shelter of such a great house, birthing babies who would grow to replace her in service once they were old enough. A life, a home and a living, with parents who would live until old age with such security. What more could anyone ask for?

It was more than Vasco could ever expect now, he told himself. A quick glance told him Gerel was still waiting for an answer. "Tell the Lord Steward I seek work. If he turns me away, then I will gladly enjoy your hospitality for a night, and tell you all I know of battles in the borderlands." He would have to censor his tale, and make the men sound more heroic than they truly were, he knew, but it wouldn't be the first time. No one wanted to hear stories of blood and death and tragedy, tainted by the darkness in his own head. If it would fill his belly for a night and perhaps the next day, he would spin tales of heroes so that those who had died in blood and pain might be remembered as more than they were in life. Perhaps it would even ease the spirits of those he had fought with, only to lose them to a stray arrow or well-placed spear.

Gerel pushed the door open wider, and beckoned him in. "Come sit in the kitchen while you wait. Cirina, the cook, will make you some tea, and maybe spare you a cake before they are sent up to the dining hall for the princesses."

To his surprise, Cirina soon had him ensconced on a seat by the fire, tea in one hand and cake in the other. Vasco hoped that Gerel was wrong and there would be a place for him in this household. He hadn't seen a single guard yet, and he didn't understand it. Surely princesses needed protection.

"The Lord Steward will see you now," Gerel said.

Vasco hurried to swallow his mouthful of cake. "Are you sure?"

She nodded, her eyes on the flagstones at her feet, as she led him out of the kitchen and into the house proper.

Tapestries lined the passageways, the colours increasingly vibrant, until they reached a richly carved door. Gerel knocked, then pushed the door open. "The man you sent for, m'lord," she said, gesturing for Vasco to enter.

The moment Vasco's worn boots touched the carpet inside the room, Gerel closed the door quietly behind him.

The Lord Steward sat in a throne-like chair raised up on a dais facing the door. Almost like a king, though the man's bald head bore no crown. His clothes were a mix of scarlet, purple and yellow silk, an eye-watering combination in any light, let alone a chamber filled with lit torches.

"What makes you think you can solve the mystery not even the king can solve?" the man asked.

Vasco bowed low, racking his brain for an answer that would satisfy the man. Something in Gerel's words struck him. "I am different to the others," he said.

The Lord Steward snorted. "Very well. You have three days to bring me a solution, or you die. I will present you to the princesses and – "

"Three days or die?" Vasco blurted out. Kun had neglected to mention this part.

And yet…

Since the day his village burned, he had gambled his life in every battle. At the end of each fighting day, either he or his enemies would lie on the battlefield to be food for crows. As a guard, he would need to be willing to lay down his life to defend his master and the master's family. How was this any different?

The Lord Steward made an impatient noise in his throat. "If I do not believe you are doing your best to uncover the mystery, it could be less than three days. My primary care is for the princesses, and if I hear a whisper of any untoward behaviour, or that you are wasting my time, your time will be up." He rose to his feet, smirking as though he liked the way he towered over Vasco from his high platform. "So, are you wasting my time now, or do you wish to meet the princesses? At one word from me, I can have you executed before you can draw breath to protest."

Vasco had no choice. At least his body would not become food for crows, and his death would be quick. Small comfort if he failed, but he did not mean to. "I would be honoured if you would present me to the ladies of the house," he said.

The man clapped his hands. "Excellent. But first, you must dress properly. The princesses will not allow you anywhere near them looking like some peasant." When Gerel cracked open the door, the Lord Steward said, "Take him to the guest dressing room and see that he is dressed."

Hoping he wouldn't have to wear the same garish colours as the Lord Steward, Vasco followed Gerel out.

Nineteen

The other girls didn't even glance up from their dinner, but Bianca couldn't tear her eyes away from the man who stepped into the room. Her fingers itched to stroke his black silk tunic. It certainly wasn't made for him

. The sleeves that would have been loose on any other man bulged with the muscles she'd seen in Kun's yard, making them look even bigger. He'd had to unlace it a little down the front to allow space for his broad chest without ripping the fabric, but the tantalising glimpse of flesh at his throat only made her mouth dry at the thought of touching, kissing, stroking…

Bianca mentally shook herself. If Cousin Efe had brought him here, dressed up like the lord she knew he wasn't, then he had a mystery to solve.

She patted the bench beside her, shifting over until her foot nudged the dog's furry body. "Come sit by me, Lord Vasco," she said, surprising herself with the low purr that came out of her throat.

Vasco looked even more startled. "I…I can't," he mumbled, backing away.

Cousin Efe screwed his face up in annoyance. "Why not? The princess gave you an order."

Vasco bowed deeply. "I am no lord, princess. I am just a common soldier, not worthy to share your table. Even the honour of sitting at your feet is more than I deserve."

Bianca couldn't help it. She laughed. "The place at my feet is taken by a dog. I'm afraid you must make do with the bench. We are not in the capital now, and the accommodations here at the Summer Palace are more informal." Her sisters were staring at her, and she felt blood rush to her cheeks. "Please sit here." She lowered her gaze until the other girls turned their attention back to their food. Evidently they hadn't noticed anything different about Vasco. They must be blind, she decided.

Vasco slid easily into the spot beside Bianca, who found her breath caught in her throat now he sat so close. Why, his thigh brushed her skirt, and if she moved her own leg just the slightest bit, she would be able to feel him through the fabric.

"I'll fetch you some wine," Hazel said, rising.

Bianca saw the reproach in her sister's gaze – after all, she was the newest to arrive, which meant she was the one who was supposed to head down to the cellar for their guest's wine – but Hazel was gone before Bianca could apologise.

Probably for the best, Bianca told herself. After all, what would Hazel say if her only excuse was that she was too busy admiring the man Cousin Efe had thrust among them? Hazel would think her mad. Perhaps she'd be right, too.

She glanced at Vasco. He sat, silent and motionless, not touching a crumb of the food that covered the table, as if he was somehow afraid of it.

"Eat something," Bianca said, offering him the nearest platter.

He bowed his head. "You first, princess."

Of course. She outranked him, something she'd forgotten in sharing a table with her sisters and the mannerless men who had come and gone.

She seized the nearest thing and took a bite, not really tasting it. Only then did Vasco take food for himself.

He ate in silence, his head down as though he

wished he were invisible.

Bianca understood the feeling, though not the reason for it. He seemed terribly uncomfortable.

"Where are you from, sir?" she asked.

He swallowed. "Nowhere."

She managed a smile. "No one is from nowhere. Why, we are all born somewhere, even if we no longer live there. Where were you born?"

"I was born in a small village that no longer exists. Razed to the ground by an advancing army. Or a retreating one. I am not sure. Heedless of those who lived there. So the village where I was born is no more, and nowhere."

His voice sounded so dead, like the village itself.

"What happened to those who lived there?" she asked.

"They died."

So final. And yet…

Hazel appeared with a jug of wine in hand, which she poured into Vasco's cup. He seized it and drank down the contents before holding the cup out for more.

"But you survived," Bianca began eagerly. "I imagine that must be a thrilling tale."

The eyes he turned to her were dark and haunted. Bianca's smile died on her lips and Hazel gave a cry of alarm. Somehow the whole jug of wine had slipped from her hand and smashed on the floor. The shards lay in a spreading lake beneath the table.

"I am sorry," Vasco said, rising. He bowed abruptly, then hurried out.

Bianca tried to follow him, but Brenna's dog tangled itself in her skirts in its hurry to reach the spilled wine, and by the time she managed to clamber to her feet, Vasco had vanished.

"Good riddance," Aruna said. "You can do much better, sister. And you will tonight."

Hazel seized her hand. "You must dance with us. I won't let you retire early. Not with that man about. He did not drink enough of the strong wine to sleep the night through. We'll take him another jug on our way to bed."

Twenty

The sweet princess with the expressive eyes just wouldn't give up. Again and again, she asked him about his home until he wanted to scream the truth for all of them to hear. The village bathed in blood, the smell of burned bodies and Dokia…Dokia…

Vasco downed his wine and pushed away from the table. He staggered out of the room, clamping his mouth shut to keep the horrors in. Like Gerel, she did not need his nightmares. They were his alone.

Speaking of nightmares, it was time to give in to his once more. He'd worked hard all day before walking up to the palace, and he could scarcely keep his eyes open. But he didn't know where his bed might be – if he even had one.

Vasco headed for the kitchen. Surely someone there would know where he was billeted.

He met Gerel on her way back to the kitchen, carrying a tray of half-eaten food.

"Serving the Lord Steward?" he asked, nodding at the scraps.

She nodded. "He takes his meals in his rooms."

"Too good for the company of princesses?" Vasco said.

Gerel reddened. "Actually, I believe they refuse to eat with him. The Lord Steward is not well liked." She pressed her lips together, as if she wished she could unsay her words.

"What about the princesses? Are they well liked?"

Gerel managed a nervous smile. "They are princesses. The king's beautiful daughters. You can't help but admire them, even if we see them so little. They spend most of their time abed, but when they are awake, they are not unkind."

Not unkind. What a thing to say about someone, let alone her mistresses. Better than not well liked, though. "What of the pale one who is fairer than the others?" he demanded.

"The Princess Bianca? She is our most recent arrival, only a few weeks ago." Gerel's expression brightened. "But I have seen more of her than her sisters combined. They sleep, while she rises early. Sometimes, she even enters the kitchen to ask for things. The way she speaks to you, looking in your eyes like she really sees you, and not just some invisible servant to be ordered about…such a small thing, but it truly sets her apart from the others. She likes to ride or walk down by the lake, and she takes a basket of provisions with her so she can stay out of the house for longer."

Remembering the time he'd seen her at Kun's cottage, Vasco asked, "Where does she ride to?"

Gerel shrugged. "Wherever she pleases, I am sure. She is a princess, and all the land around belongs to her father, the king. Who would dare stop her?"

Who indeed. "Do you know anything about this mystery with the shoes?" he said.

Gerel shook her head. "No more than you. That is why you sleep in the maid's room off their bedchamber, and not one of us."

He had a place to sleep. Vasco grasped at the idea. "Can you show me where?" he asked urgently.

"Of course. I have already placed your things there. You left them in the kitchen." Gerel glanced down. "Let me just take this tray to the kitchen, and I will show you up."

Gerel returned a moment later, beckoning Vasco to follow her.

Tapestries lined the walls here, too, but they were not as grand as the ones outside the Lord Steward's rooms. They looked too old and faded to be the princesses' own work.

The décor didn't improve when they entered the princesses' receiving chamber. If anything, the walls were even more bare here, for the room held only a few benches and little else. The girls did not spend much time here.

Gerel gestured toward an open door at the other end of the chamber. This new room was full of beds — a dozen to be precise. All the princesses slept in the same room, which had a row of small windows, but only the one door in or out. Perhaps they danced around their audience chamber and that's why there was no furniture to speak of. Mystery solved.

"Your bed is there." Gerel pointed at an alcove just outside the door to the princesses' bedchamber. It contained a straw pallet and some hooks that now held his meagre belongings. "You have the most beautiful cloak."

Vasco glanced at Kun's gift. In truth, the thick, black wool was better quality than anything he'd ever owned, but much like tonight's fancy clothes, he hadn't been able to refuse it. He didn't have to sleep in silk, though. But Gerel should go before he undressed.

"I wish to retire now," he said.

It took Gerel a moment before she understood. Then she coloured. "Of course. In the morning, when you wish to break your fast, come down to the kitchen. We have orders to serve you in the dining chamber with the princesses, but they rise so late that you might wish for something earlier." She bobbed on the spot, as if she'd almost curtsied to him before remembering she didn't need to, and hurried off.

Vasco peeled off the black silk fripperies the Lord Steward had made him wear, and donned one of his own worn tunics. Much more comfortable, he stretched out on his bed and almost instantly fell asleep.

Twenty-One

While Bianca's sisters headed for their bedchamber, she dutifully made her way down to the cellar for another jug of wine. On her way back up, she returned to the dining hall to grab Vasco's cup from the table. She peered under the table, wondering what to do about the puddle of wine. She decided to leave it for one of the servants to deal with. After all, someone would come to clear the table of the remains of their meal.

Most of the wine was gone, sunk between the flagstones or, more likely, lapped up by the little dog that now slept under the table in the puddle that remained. Bianca smiled. Brenna's dog would probably sleep there all night.

Wine jug in one hand, cup in the other, she made her way to her bedchamber. Efe waited outside, looking irritable. "Hurry up. I must lock the door," he said, waving her in.

Lock the door? Bianca had never seen him do such a thing before. She stepped into the audience chamber, then turned to ask Efe what he meant by it. He slammed the door shut in her face and she heard the sounds of a bolt being drawn across it, effectively locking them all in. Including Vasco, she realised, who now slept soundly on the pallet beside their bedchamber door.

No wine necessary.

Nevertheless, she set the cup and jug down beside his bed. Staring at the snoring soldier, she suddenly felt very tired herself. Probably because she'd slept so little the previous night. Maybe she should climb into bed and sleep the night away. Her sisters' shoe mystery could wait for another night.

"Hurry up and dress, or we shall be late!" Nera hissed, tugging on Bianca's arm.

She allowed herself to be pulled into the bedchamber. Brenna closed the door behind her. All the other girls were in various stages of dressing not for bed but for what appeared to be a royal ball. Well, if they were going to dance, she thought wryly, why not? They might be exiled from the palace and the capital, but they could still dress like they were attending court.

Now, more than ever, she felt too tired to join them.

"Hurry!" Nera repeated as Hazel helped her lace up her gown.

Bianca shook her head. "I am too tired. Tomorrow night, maybe. I can scarcely keep my eyes open."

Nera made an exasperated noise. "Sleep, then. We'll choose the handsomest and you'll have to make do with what is left. Unless you prefer the fool outside?" She tittered, and the other girls joined in.

And what if she did? Bianca wanted to say, but she held her tongue. They were locked in their own bedchamber, with no men, handsome or otherwise. She stripped down to her shift and climbed beneath the covers of her bed. Almost as soon as her head touched the pillow, she drifted off into dreams.

What seemed like only a moment later, she was roused by the sound of hammering on her bedchamber door.

Twenty-Two

Vasco woke with a start. It took him a moment to realise that the soft weight on top of him was merely the bed coverings, and not Dokia's dead body. He wasn't sure which nightmares were worse – the ones in the heat of battle, or the ones from the night his village burned. He hoped he hadn't woken the princesses by crying out.

He rose and padded to the door to their bedchamber, pressing his ear to the closed door. Silence greeted him – they were surely asleep. Sighing in relief, he crossed to the narrow window and took a deep breath of the cool night air, hoping it would clear his head. But the view from the window made his breath catch in his throat.

A flotilla of small boats, like a flock of swans, drifted across the lake toward the misty island in the middle. Moonlight glistened on silk and he realised what he was seeing – in each boat sat a princess, wearing a shimmering silk gown and, he didn't doubt, a pair of matching slippers that would be danced to pieces by morning. He shouted, but no one seemed to hear him.

He had to follow them. Vasco dashed for the door to the passage, only to find it barred from the outside. He was locked in.

But if he was locked in…surely they had been, too. There must be another way out – through their bedchamber, perhaps.

He tried that door, but it was locked, too. He hammered on it, then threw his weight against the timber, over and over again. He had to follow them. His very life depended on it.

He heard the scrape of a bolt and the door cracked open. "What is it?" a sleepy female voice asked.

Had he imagined the boats? If the princesses were still in their bedchamber, he couldn't have seen them on the lake. Vasco pushed the door wide and strode into the room. A candle burned beside one of the empty beds, but there was not a girl to be seen.

He swore.

"What does that mean?" a female voice asked.

Vasco blinked. Beside the door stood Bianca, wearing nothing but a thin shift, as if she'd been roused from her bed. Shame welled up as he realised he'd been the one to wake her in his panic.

"Forgive me, princess," he said awkwardly. "I had a bad dream, and then I thought I saw something on the lake."

"On the lake?" Princess Bianca crossed to the window beside his bed and peered out. "I don't see anything."

Vasco looked over her shoulder. The boats had reached the mist, which hid them from view. Yet he knew what he'd seen.

"Maybe I dreamed that, too," he admitted.

"When I had troubling dreams as a child, my mother would have one of the maids bring me milk to drink. Ice-cold from the cellars." Bianca smiled at the memory. "I can send for some, if you like?"

Vasco shook his head. "The door is bolted. We are locked in. Though how your sisters managed to get out…I don't know." He wanted to ask her what she knew, but he already felt embarrassed enough. Interrogating a princess was hardly the way to behave after he had woken her so rudely.

"Wine, then?" she asked, offering the jug.

Kun had warned him not to drink the wine. "NO!"

he said, then added, "It might dull my wits. I will need all the wits I have to solve this mystery. Is there anything you can tell me about it, princess?"

Sadly, Bianca shook her head. "I don't know where they go. Until tonight, I didn't believe they went anywhere at all, yet they have gone. And tomorrow there will be a pile of shoes on the threshold of our room for me to trip over."

Vasco managed a smile. "A graceful princess like yourself would never do something so clumsy."

Bianca laughed so hard she had to sit down. "I am many things, but graceful isn't one of them. As you will soon find out, if you spend much time with me."

"I have only three days," he replied. Three days left to live, unless he found a way to follow the princesses across the lake. But he didn't tell Bianca that, for he would sound like a whining coward, when he was neither. If he would die for his failure, so be it.

She sighed. "So you do." She glanced up. "Perhaps tomorrow night you should hide in our bedchamber, so you can see where they go. Wearing your new cloak, you will be invisible in the shadows." She reached out to touch the wool cloak Kun had given him. In fact, her words echoed Kun's almost exactly.

Yet she looked the polar opposite of the old witch. Where Kun wore so many layers of clothing she appeared shapeless, Bianca wore a thin shift that clung to her curves even as it concealed them, but barely. She truly was the most beautiful woman he had ever seen, and in the moonlight shining through the window, she seemed infused with a kind of magic that turned her from a woman into a goddess. The kind armies would die for.

Yet she was still a woman, as much as he was a man. Increasingly aware of how little clothing they wore and how much his body desired her, he forced himself to shut down all such thoughts. She was a princess, which made her untouchable by one such as him. That she spoke to him at all was an honour he did not deserve.

"Perhaps I will. It's too late for that tonight, though. It appears our birds have flown," he said. He bowed. "I am sorry I woke you, princess. It will not happen again."

She rose, unwittingly giving him a glimpse down the front of her shift before she straightened. Vasco had to close his eyes, but it was too late. Those creamy breasts would haunt his dreams until the day he died.

In three days.

"Pleasant dreams, Vasco," she said.

He didn't reply.

Twenty-Three

Day dawned and Bianca rose with the sun, as usual. Her sisters had returned and they were sound asleep, having left the usual pile of shoes before the door, which she stepped over carefully. She didn't want to trip and wake Vasco.

When she reached the receiving room, she found his bed empty and the outer door ajar. She needn't have bothered being quiet. For a moment, she worried that he might have left, but his belongings still hung from the hooks over his bed. Perhaps he was simply breaking his fast, she decided. Something she should do, too.

Maybe they could speak more over the morning

meal. After all, it wasn't like her sisters would be joining them. She would have him all to herself.

She fairly skipped down to the kitchen to order breakfast, before asking about Vasco's whereabouts.

"Out by the archery butts," she was told.

Bianca knew the spot, though she'd never seen anyone using them. The practice targets stood on the lakeshore, faded from long disuse.

As she approached, she heard the whistle and thunk of arrows hitting a target in quick succession. It wasn't until she stepped out onto the sand that she realised how good a marksman he was. The targets were at least a hundred yards away, maybe more, yet he never missed. In fact, one target was peppered with so many arrows it had split in two, and the one beside it looked dangerously close to sharing its fate.

"You are an exceptional shot, Vasco. Wherever did you learn to shoot?" she called.

The next arrow sheared off into the water as Vasco started in surprise. He recovered quickly. "Good morning, princess. My father taught me to shoot a bow when I was a small boy, and it became a part of daily training when I joined the army. An infantryman who cannot shoot becomes a target for those who can." He winced as if at a painful memory.

"From seeing how well you shoot, I imagine you

have killed many men with your well-placed arrows," Bianca said.

Vasco sighed. "Then you imagine wrong." He set down his bow and trudged out of earshot to retrieve his arrows. He took his time, as though he hoped she might grow bored and leave, but she had learned early in her life that boredom was best chased away by a busy mind when it belonged to a girl in a harem, lest she go completely mad at the tedium of her own life. Some of her father's wives and concubines had succumbed to madness, and taken their own lives, she knew, though her mother had considered her too young to hear of such things.

Watching him walk away from her, Bianca realised he limped, favouring his left leg. For all her days of watching him, she'd never seen him limping before.

When he returned with his arms full of arrows, she asked, "Did you fall from the roof and injure yourself while you were fixing Kun's house?"

Vasco frowned. "No, I did not."

"Then why are you limping?" she persisted.

He slid his arrows back into their quiver. "Because in the heat of battle, someone shot me with an arrow that I will carry with me always." He patted his knee, shouldered both quivers and his bow, then headed for the house.

"That is hardly fair," Bianca said, hurrying to catch

up. For a lame man, he moved quite fast.

He laughed without humour. "Princess, war is never fair. Good men die and bad men live on, unhurt. And then there are those like me who perhaps should have died from their wounds, who yet survive, as if fate has yet to make up its mind about me. When your business is war, you live from day to day, meal to meal, one battle to the next until it is your last. I am not a shoemaker, piecing together pretty things for your feet. My job was to destroy. Men and lives and property – whatever got in my commander's way. Perhaps I am no longer a good man at all, but a bad one, after all the things I have done."

No. She refused to believe it. "You built Kun a new barn, and rebuilt her house. That is not destruction."

"There are dozens of dead trees now filling her woodshed that would call you a liar, if they but had mouths to speak," Vasco said. "My axe no longer cuts down men, but it still thirsts for death."

Bianca stopped dead. Had she truly been so stupid not to see it?

"You mean you've hurt women? And you will again?" she asked, hating how weak her voice sounded.

"NO! I have never intentionally hurt a woman, and I never intend to. I have made mistakes, but..." He shook his head. "Never mind. My troubles are so far beneath you as to be completely insignificant. Please forget I said it." He redoubled his pace back to the house.

"What was her name?" Bianca demanded. "The woman who was hurt because of your mistake?"

Vasco stopped so suddenly she almost ran into him. He whirled on the spot, eyeing her as if sizing her up. "Eudokia. If she had lived, she would be my wife."

Bianca's heart ached for him. "I am sorry for your loss," she said carefully. "I hope she sees the honour you do your family now that she walks among the ancestors."

Vasco's mouth twisted into a wry smile. "Given her memory disturbs my sleep and drives me to practice shooting even when I no longer have anyone to shoot at, perhaps the honour belongs to her. She was a good girl, and a kind one, who did not deserve to die the way she did."

"How did she die?" Bianca ventured.

"Horribly. Painfully. Perhaps even cursing my name. I can only guess, for I did not see her die." Vasco's eyes seemed to focus on her properly. "My apologies, princess. You do not need to hear of such things. Have you broken your fast yet? Gerel said she would summon me when the food was ready."

Horribly. Painfully. And in the next breath, he spoke of one of the palace servants, as if the death of the woman he loved was something he could easily dismiss. Palace servants he could name, though he had only arrived last night.

Bianca didn't know what to make of the man. He was certainly different to the others, but…had she made a terrible mistake and invited a killer into her home?

Twenty-Four

The princess seemed a lot more human in daylight. More like an innocent young woman who had lived a sheltered but privileged life in the palace than last night's moonlit vision.

Yet she'd managed to make him speak Dokia's name aloud for the first time since the day she died. There was just something about her...

Something that made him follow her into the house and to the dining hall, to share a meal with her instead of heading for the kitchen and the servants' table, where men of his rank belonged. She smiled at him as she sat across from him, for all the world like they were equals, and his heart warmed at her welcome.

She is a princess and I am nothing, he reminded himself, tucking his boots under the table, but they bumped into something. He peered into the shadows. "Does your dog normally sleep under the table?" he asked.

"He's not my dog. He belongs to my sister, Brenna. I don't know where he usually sleeps, but last night I think he drank too much wine, and drifted off into sleep where he lay." She broke off a piece of meat and tossed it before the animal's nose. "Wake up, boy. Food for you."

The dog didn't move.

She nudged the animal with one slippered foot, but it didn't respond. Puzzled, she reached a hand under the table to stroke the dog. The moment her fingers touched its fur, she snatched her hand back as if scalded. "He's cold," she said, her eyes widening with horror.

Vasco dragged the bench back and crawled beneath the table. He scooped up the dog's limp body and set it on the bench. After a quick examination, he confirmed his first verdict. "The dog is dead. He must have died in his sleep, he appears so peaceful."

A tear slid down Bianca's cheek as she shook her head. "Oh, I told Brenna wine was bad for dogs. He drank too much and it poisoned him, I know it!"

Poison. The thought chilled him to the bone.

Poison was a woman's weapon, like an axe was his. "I've seen men die from drinking too much liquor. This looks like some other poison."

"But who would poison a defenceless dog?" the princess whispered. "It makes no sense."

"Perhaps the dog wasn't the intended victim," Vasco said gravely. "What did he eat last night?"

"I don't know," she said tearfully. "I only know he drank the wine before he fell asleep."

The wine. Wine one of the girls had poured into his cup, before he bumped her and spilled it on the floor. No wonder Kun had told him not to drink the wine, if it was poisoned.

"Who drank the wine last night?" he demanded.

Bianca stared at him. "None of us. I mean, we do not…the wine is Cousin Efe's, from the cellars. Only at very special celebrations do we have wine, but it's not the same. Ours is lighter and sweeter and…"

Vasco huffed out a breath at his own stupidity. He'd drunk poisoned wine, despite Kun's warning. He was lucky to be alive. "So just me and the dog, hm?"

Bianca's mouth dropped open. "You don't think…" She looked genuinely horrified.

Either she was very good at looking innocent, or she hadn't known about the poison. She hadn't fetched or poured the wine, though – that had been one of her sisters. One of the same sisters who had disappeared across the lake last night.

Bianca's thoughts seemed to be travelling along the same path as his own. "No, Hazel would not poison your wine. She taps it from the same barrel in the cellar. I have done it myself. It is Cousin Efe's strongest vintage, and it helps one sleep, Hazel says. If there is poison in the wine, then it is in the barrel."

Vasco said nothing.

"I'll take you down there and show you the barrel myself!" Bianca insisted. She marched to the door, then turned. "Are you coming?"

For a moment, he had forgotten that this pretty princess was the daughter of a king. A king whose desire for conquest was the reason half the world was at war. Bemused, he rose to his feet. "Of course, princess."

As he followed her into the cellars, it dawned on him that if she were to order his death, he would perish. The Lord Steward might hold more power than Vasco himself would ever possess, but Princess Bianca was one of the twelve mistresses of this palace.

He could always ask one of her sisters about the wine but…

But Kun had told him to ask Bianca for help if he ran into trouble. None of the others.

Vasco shook his head in an attempt to clear it. Solving mysteries and playing politics were tasks for a noble courtier, not a farm boy turned soldier. If he survived the next three days, he'd beg the king for a job as a simple guardsman. One who manned the gate or the wall and did as he was told.

"That barrel!" Bianca pointed.

Vasco hid a smile. The princess couldn't tell one cask from another. The hogshead she indicated stood out among the massive tuns filling the rest of the wine cellar, for it was the only cask of its size in the place. He found a bowl and filled it with wine.

Cautiously, he sniffed it, but it smelled of…wine. He wasn't sure what poison smelled or tasted like. All he knew was that it could kill.

"Are there rats in this cellar?" he asked.

Bianca's eyes grew wide. "Rats?" She edged toward the steps.

Ah, yes. He'd forgotten how much rats had frightened the women of his village. He'd only ever brought one home as a pet and his mother had screamed herself hoarse.

"All cellars have rats," he said with what he hoped was an air of authority. He hoped he was right, too. "We'll leave this bowl out for them, and come back this evening. If the wine is poisoned, then we will know."

Bianca bit her lip and nodded.

Vasco let out a breath he hadn't known he was

holding. By the ancestors, he was truly stumbling in the dark now.

He followed Bianca up into the palace proper, where they were met by Gerel. "Is there anything you wanted, mistress?" she asked Bianca.

Bianca glanced at Vasco, then said, "We were looking for the Lord Steward's wine."

Gerel smiled. "Most of the wine in this cellar is his. He drinks only wine with the Gu mark." She touched the brush marks on the lid of the nearest tun. "Like this."

Vasco traced the lines that made up the complicated symbol until he thought he could recognise it. He spotted it on several other casks, while others bore other marks he didn't know, but when he reached the hogshead, he found no mark at all. Only a bird, branded into the lid. "So the Lord Steward doesn't drink from this cask?" Vasco asked.

Gerel peered at it. "No. I have never served that to anyone."

Vasco wanted to ask more, but Bianca's cold voice silenced him.

"Thank you. You may go," Bianca said, waving the serving girl away.

Gerel bobbed on the spot and hurried off.

When the maid was out of sight, Bianca's regal stance slumped. "This is the wine my sisters told me to fetch for the men who seek to solve the shoe mystery. They believed they were siphoning it from Cousin Efe's private supplies. But if it is poisoned, and all those men have been drinking it…what happened to them?"

Three days. Three days was all they had before… "They died, princess."

She clapped her hands to her mouth. "No! Surely not. They leave. They leave the palace, never to return…" Her eyes begged him to take the words back.

"They die, because they failed. As will I." He wanted to reassure her with all his being, but he could not lie to her. "The Lord Steward said I have three days to solve your mystery, or I die. Whether they died by poison or something else, it won't change the result. Men are dying to protect your sisters' secret. Is it worth their lives, princess?"

"No," she whispered, tears running down her cheeks.

"So tell me where they go," he said.

She shook her head. "I can't. Ancestors help me, Vasco, but I cannot tell you what I do not know!" She broke into a run, dashing up the steps and away.

Vasco was tempted to follow her, but he resisted. If she wanted him, she could send a servant to summon him, and he would obey.

Or he could wait until tonight, don his new cloak, and hide in the princesses' bedchamber. When they opened their secret entrance, he would follow them across the lake and uncover their secret. His life depended on it.

Twenty-Five

Bianca walked the lake trails without seeing them, her mind roiling with more and more terrible possibilities. Her sisters were poisoning people. The adventurers they'd sneered at might have been fools, but that didn't mean they deserved to die for it.

Brenna would be heartbroken when she learned of her dog's death.

Vasco would die if Bianca didn't help him. And his death would be her fault, because she had insisted on inviting him to the palace.

When she thought it was late enough to wake her sisters, she headed into the house. Afternoon sun filtered through the windows in their bedchamber, and the girls showed signs of stirring.

"Brenna's dog is dead," Bianca announced.

"My…what?" Brenna mumbled.

"Your dog is dead. We think the wine is poisoned," Bianca said.

Nera peered at her blearily. "Who's we?"

Bianca cursed her ill-chosen words. "I do. And…Vasco. The man who arrived last night."

Nera sat up suddenly. "You stayed here to flirt with one of Cousin Efe's adventurers? Ugh. Tonight, if we have to drag you all the way there, you are coming dancing with us."

Dancing. The one thing Bianca hated most. But if it would save Vasco's life…she must do it.

"All right," she said.

"How could the wine be poisoned?" Hazel asked. "I took it from the barrel myself. No one touched it but me. You don't think that I tried to kill Brenna's dog, do you?"

"Of course not," Bianca said. "If anything, the whole barrel is poisoned."

"Then why hasn't Cousin Efe expired yet?" Aruna grumbled.

"He doesn't drink from that barrel. I checked with the servants. The wine we've been giving those poor fools was poisoned," Bianca said.

"But it hasn't killed any of them," Hazel objected.

"They drink it down like it was water, and you can hear them snoring all night. Only Brenna's dear little dog has died. Perhaps it is only deadly to dogs."

Bianca doubted it, but, "Perhaps," she admitted. Best not to argue with her sisters now. Not when she would soon have to betray them to save a man's life.

Twenty-Six

When he heard the babble of female voices approaching, Vasco's courage failed. Instead of huddling in the corner of their bedchamber under his cloak, he dived under the nearest bed. A bed with a sword beneath it, of all things.

Trying to keep himself concealed and quiet while the princesses bustled about was bad enough, until the purple gown he'd seen Bianca wearing only hours before puddled on the floor inches from his face. He couldn't help himself. A glance upwards revealed pale, shapely legs and the underside of the sweetest pair of breasts he'd ever seen. Ancestors help him, but even Dokia's couldn't compare.

Vasco squeezed his eyes shut, but it was too late. The image of Princess Bianca's naked body was branded to the inside of his eyelids. Princess or not, the burning desire that coursed through his body didn't care – he wanted her in every way a man wanted a woman.

He forced himself to think of the dead rats he'd found in the cellar this evening. Rats that had drunk the poisoned wine and died for their crimes.

The slither of silk made him open his eyes again. The purple gown was replaced by one as blue as a summer sky, covering those beautiful legs to the ankle. A pair of matching slippers, embroidered in gold so pale it matched her hair, slapped to the floor. She carefully slid her feet into them.

"Have you seen tonight's fool? He's not in his bed," one of the girls said.

"Not since last night. Perhaps he has given up." The second girl giggled.

A third voice piped up: "Or perhaps he is hiding in this very chamber, thinking to follow us. Search the room!"

Bianca bent over, her face so close to Vasco's that he could feel her breath on his face. Then she brushed his hood forward, covering his face entirely. "Melania, where would he hide? He would need some sort of magic in order to conceal himself in here. If you want to search the room, suit yourself. The rest of us have more important things to do. Like dressing our hair."

"Let me do yours, Bianca!" one of the girls begged.

To Vasco's surprise, he found he could see through the cloak as though it were gossamer thin, instead of thick wool. When an angry face framed with dark hair peered under the bed, he saw her as clearly as he'd seen Bianca. Yet she shook her head in annoyance and moved to the next bed as if she hadn't seen him.

Vasco breathed a sigh of relief.

"Come on, girls. I can see the boats!" a princess called imperiously.

A dozen pairs of feet clad in dancing slippers stampeded to the corner of the room furthest from the windows, where a section of the stone floor tilted up at a strange angle. It was a trapdoor, Vasco realised, with a thin veneer of stone on top to make it look like a normal part of the flagstones. One by one, the girls descended through the hole in the floor.

Crawling out from under the bed, he tried to stay low so they wouldn't see him. He rounded the end of the last bed, only to see the trapdoor closing behind the last princess.

He dived for it, hands outstretched, but he wasn't quick enough. The trapdoor settled among the flagstones as if it had never been. Vasco raked his nails across the stones, to no avail. He didn't know the trick to opening the secret door.

He sat back on his heels, anger and despair warring within him. He should have been faster. Now he would waste another night.

As if by magic, the trapdoor rose.

"What are you doing?" Melania's voice demanded.

"I forgot my fan," Bianca said.

That was all the warning Vasco got before the trapdoor was thrown open and she burst out of the hole in the floor. She raced past him as if she couldn't see him, presumably in search of her fan.

Vasco took his chance and propelled himself through the hole in the floor. Rough steps had been cut into the stone, leading down into the darkness. With one hand on the damp, stone wall, he followed them down to where he could see a light flickering.

One of the princesses held a torch aloft, her face scrunched up in annoyance. "Do we have to wait for her?" the dark-haired girl, Melania, asked.

Another girl put a hand on her shoulder. "Yes, we do. It will take all of us to break the curse. Without her, we are only eleven. The spell calls for twelve princesses to free the twelve princes. Any fewer and they will still be trapped."

Melania grumbled something under her breath, then fell silent.

"I'm coming!" Bianca called from above.

All eyes suddenly turned toward Vasco, too quickly for him to hide, yet none of the girls reacted to the sight of him. They continued to stare expectantly at the steps behind him.

Figuring that the torch had blinded them so much that they couldn't see him, Vasco relaxed. It was only a moment before Bianca came down the steps, painted fan in one hand and a candle in the other. She walked to his side, so close she brushed his cloak, and waved the fan at her sisters. "See? I told you I would be quick. Ooh, are those the boats?"

As one, the girls turned away from her to stare at the lake.

Vasco couldn't believe none of the girls had seen him. Not even Bianca, and she'd touched him. Perhaps the cloak truly did make him invisible, like Kun had said. Still, it wouldn't do to be reckless. He waited for Bianca and her candle to lead the way before he followed, several steps behind.

The stone path was uneven and he stumbled frequently, wishing he dared to walk closer to the light she held. If only the world were a different place, where a soldier could walk arm in arm with a princess as equals. But it was not to be.

His distraction was almost his undoing. The path curved, but he had not seen it, and he fell headlong over a pile of rocks. The cloak's hood slipped from his head.

A moment later, Bianca cried out, "My light!"

The candle rolled down the path toward Vasco. Impossibly, the flame hadn't been extinguished. Which meant that if Bianca came chasing it, she would spot him instantly.

Vasco forced himself to his feet, pulling the cloak closed around him once more, as the candle came to a stop where he had lain only moments before. He edged along the path, which was scarcely wide enough for one, let alone two.

Bianca rounded the corner, too intent on her candle to notice her cloak brushing against his.

Vasco experienced a mad desire to reach out and wrap his arms around her, bringing her body against his and…then what? She would hardly consent to a kiss. He clenched his hands at his sides to stop himself from doing something else stupid.

"Must hurry…don't want to miss the boat," she murmured to herself as she passed.

Though he was certain the words weren't for him, Vasco obeyed them anyway, stumbling down the path to reach the other girls. More confident in his invisibility, he dared to stand closer than before.

"What is she doing? They are almost here!" Melania muttered.

Vasco followed the girl's gaze to the lake. The same

boats he had seen vanish into the mist the previous night now approached the shore. A lantern hung at one end, while a dark-cloaked figure poled the boat at the other end.

The hair on the back of Vasco's neck prickled. Whoever was concealed by those cloaks brought an ill wind with them.

The first of the boats reached the shore and its captain leaped onto the sand, holding onto the lantern post so that the boat did not drift away. He let his hood fall back, revealing hair as long and pale as Bianca's. "Good evening, my beautiful princesses." He flashed a brilliant smile before bowing low. "Is it true that there are twelve of you this evening?" The eagerness in his tone set Vasco's teeth on edge.

"We were twelve, but Bianca ran back to get something," Melania grumbled.

"I am here!" Bianca's voice called.

Vasco wanted to move to the middle of the path to bar her way. Nothing good would come of this, he was certain of it. He must protect her.

The other girls closed around her, a gaggle of impenetrable geese, until they delivered her to the cloaked man.

"This is Bianca, newly arrived among us," Brenna said, pushing her forward. "With her, we are twelve."

"Such beauty," the man breathed, reaching for

Bianca's hand. He bowed low over it. "Princess Bianca, I am Prince Corbin, and it would be my honour to be your escort tonight."

"But I thought I was going to – " Melania protested before Brenna hushed her.

"She would be delighted," Brenna said. "You have rendered her speechless, Prince Corbin. Bianca has spent all her life in the women's palace, where we see few men, but I am sure you will help her find her voice again."

Bianca had no trouble speaking to men, Vasco wanted to say, incensed at her sister's presumption, but once again, he was silenced by Bianca herself.

"I thank you, sir," she said, accepting his assistance into the boat.

More boats had come ashore during the exchange, and the girls spread out along the beach, one to a boat.

Corbin had already poled Bianca's boat away from shore – too far for Vasco to reach them. He cast about for another boat to board.

"You'll do as you're told," Brenna hissed as she shoved Melania toward one of the boats. "Prince Fiachra is just as handsome as his brother. You should consider yourself lucky to have a suitor at all. Why, your mother was a slave before my father took her for a concubine."

While Melania struggled and whined about her

mother, Vasco crept into the boat Brenna evidently had in mind for the irritating girl. The cloaked man who stood beside it – Fiachra, Vasco presumed – only had eyes for Melania. The hunger in his gaze made Vasco feel queasy.

At a nod from Brenna, Fiachra seized the slight girl and deposited her in the boat, narrowly missing Vasco. Fiachra stepped aboard after her and quickly poled the boat out into deeper water.

Once again, the boats headed for the small, mist-shrouded island in the middle of the lake. Only this time, Vasco was with them.

Twenty-Seven

Bianca wasn't entirely sure what to make of Prince Corbin. Between his perfect manners, outrageous compliments and the glittering coronet he wore on his head beneath the hood, he appeared to be the sort of prince only found in fairytales.

He was the complete opposite of all the men who'd come to the Summer Palace, trying to solve her sisters' mystery. Yes, even the opposite of Vasco. Where Vasco said little and behaved as though he felt he was out of place, Corbin smiled and laughed as if he was completely comfortable.

On a misty lake, late at night, carrying off a princess whose father would probably skin him alive if he caught Corbin, the man's smile never wavered until they reached their destination – the small island in the middle of the lake.

As he helped her out of the boat, Bianca glanced back. The Summer Palace wasn't visible through the mist. So close, and yet so far. She shivered.

"I should get you inside. It is warmer there," Corbin said, offering his arm. In his free hand, he held the lantern from the boat.

Without his help and the light, she was bound to trip again, Bianca knew, so she tucked her hand into the crook of his elbow and allowed him to lead her away from the water.

Another boat crunched into the shore behind her, but Bianca's attention was drawn to the path ahead. Corbin led her up a slight rise to the bare peak of a hill, the highest point on the island. Torches glowed and danced in a circle around them as Corbin set down his lantern.

He reached down, grasped a ring set in a stone and heaved. It came up easily, tilting up to reveal that the slice of rock was fixed to a wooden trapdoor, the twin of the one in her bedchamber. Almost as though the same person had constructed them both. Though to what end?

"You look intrigued, princess. Wait until you see what awaits you downstairs," Corbin declared, gesturing for her to precede him.

Descending into a dark cellar with a stranger didn't seem like the wisest thing to do, but a glance back told Bianca that her sisters and their cloaked escorts were on their way here. They didn't look worried.

She stepped inside, holding tight to the railing as she followed the steep spiral staircase down, down, down until she was certain she was below the surface of the lake. Yet the deeper she descended, the brighter it became. The mystery was solved when she rounded the last twist into a small subterranean chamber filled with candles.

Corbin was only a few steps behind her. "Let me take your cloak, princess."

As he spoke, she was already unfastening the clasp, so it was a simple matter to shrug the garment off into his waiting arms. Bianca patted her hair carefully and straightened her dress, wishing she had thought to bring a mirror instead of a fan.

Corbin finished hanging her cloak up next to his, and turned to face her. He immediately dropped to his knees. "Princess Bianca, never have I seen such radiant beauty. You are an angel come to earth to tempt me, surely. I will not rest until you agree to be my wife."

What? Bianca searched his expression for some hint that he was joking, for surely this was a jest. No man declared his love for a girl the moment he met her.

And no sane woman would accept the proposal of such a fool.

And yet…the look in his eyes was so earnest, she was forced to believe he meant every word.

"I…am speechless once more," she faltered.

"Beautiful Bianca, I understand. Take all the time you wish. But do not torture me for too long. I will not be willing to let you go tonight until I have received your answer." Something flickered in his eyes so quickly Bianca wasn't sure whether she'd imagined it or not. Whatever it was, it chilled her, for his words definitely carried a threat.

What would he do if she refused him? Would he hold her prisoner here until she changed her mind?

Aruna stepped off the bottom stair and allowed her princely escort – he wore a circlet, too, though of a different design to Corbin's – to divest her of her cloak. She received no marriage proposal. Her escort merely extended his arm to her and they walked together through the arched doorway at the other end of the room.

More people spilled down the stairs, crowding the tiny room.

"Allow me to show you our humble home," Corbin said with a wry smile.

He led her through the arch Aruna had entered. Only, it wasn't just an arch – it was an arched passageway that extended a considerable distance. From what Bianca had seen of the island above, she was certain this passage extended under the lake itself. Why, it felt like they were walking back to the palace, it was so long.

Finally, they stepped out into a much wider space. Bianca's breath caught in her throat.

The domed ballroom stretched high above them, the ceiling made of… "Is that glass?" she asked eagerly, craning her neck to stare up at it. Each pane was no bigger than her mirror at home, but each pane was a slightly different colour, turning the ceiling into a marvellous mosaic that shone in the moonlight filtering through the lake.

"It is," Corbin replied, grinning. "Brought from Arabia just to build this ballroom. I swear some magic must have gone into its construction, for it is only by some miracle that the lake doesn't try to claim our home for its own."

As if by magic, music began to play.

"Shall we dance, princess?" Corbin asked.

Now Bianca truly was speechless. At her father's court, the only dances she'd heard of were performed by women, for the pleasure of men, and no man ever danced with a woman. It was unheard of. "I…don't know how," she said.

He laughed. "I will soon teach you. You will see.

Your sisters said the same thing to my brothers, and watch them now!"

Brenna, then Aruna, Nera, Hazel…all of her sisters had entered the ballroom while she'd been admiring the ceiling, and each stood in the embrace of a different prince, moving about the dance floor in what looked like synchronised steps. Well, nearly synchronised. Melania kept twisting in her partner's arms so that she could glare at Bianca.

Bianca sighed. She hoped when Corbin lost patience with her for her lack of dancing skills, he would rescind his marriage proposal and consent to let her go home.

Twenty-Eight

"Something pulled on my cloak, I swear it!" Nera cried.

Vasco swore under his breath and lifted his foot off her cloak. If she hadn't let it trail on the ground behind her, he would not have trodden on it.

"You must have caught it on a branch or something," Brenna advised her. Even though she looked in Vasco's direction, he was certain she could not see him. None of the girls could, and none of their mysterious princes, either.

Nera seemed satisfied by Brenna's explanation, but it drew Vasco's attention to the well-worn path at their feet, which had no branches to catch anyone's clothes, and the trees that grew on either side. Their leaves shone silver in the moonlight, as though made of metal and not living wood. He hadn't seen any such trees when he was cutting timber for Kun's cottage. Without thinking, he broke off a small branch so that he might study it later, in daylight.

"What was that?" Hazel whispered. "I heard something crack."

"Someone stepped on a stick, is all," Brenna replied. "Why, I think I felt one crunch under my shoe just a moment ago."

One by one, the young couples disappeared into a hole at the top of the hill. Fortunately for Vasco, the last one left the trapdoor open, so he climbed in after them.

At the bottom of the stairs, they were too preoccupied with uncloaking and flirting to notice him slipping through the crowd, though he brushed against more than one person on his way through. He passed through the passage, marvelling that he cast no shadow. He truly was invisible.

More confident now, he strode into the ballroom, keeping close to the walls. He watched Bianca talking and laughing with the prince as easily as she'd done with him that morning. What he didn't like was the adoration in the prince's eyes, burning brighter every moment he spent with her.

When the prince asked her to dance and actually dared to hold her in his arms, Vasco felt his fury rise. How dare any man put his hands on her? He wasn't worthy to touch her!

Even as he started forward to yank the man away from her, Vasco's own mind ventured a traitorous thought: why couldn't a prince touch a princess? Vasco might not be worthy of her, but she belonged with a prince, a man of her own rank. Reluctantly, he shrank back against the wall, forcing himself to watch but not interfere.

Even if it killed him.

After some time dancing, the prince led Bianca to a table where food and wine was laid out. He poured the wine into what looked like a golden goblet, before handing it to her.

After last night's poisoned wine, he wanted to leap forward and dash the cup from her hands, but she simply sipped from it and smiled.

Vasco crept closer, in order to hear their conversation.

Another couple joined them before he could reach them.

"So how are you two getting along?" Brenna asked as her prince poured her wine.

"I don't think I have ever done so much dancing in my life!" Bianca said.

"She dances as well on the dance floor as she does around my heart. I have made her an offer of marriage, but she will not give me an answer." Corbin gave a melancholy sigh.

Vasco's heart stuttered. Surely he hadn't heard correctly. The prince had proposed to marry her?

"You will say yes, won't you?" Brenna implored. "We have all agreed to marry one of the princes. Once you accept Corbin, that will be all of us." She beamed.

Bianca lowered her gaze. "But I scarcely know him."

Vasco's heart began to beat again. The man might have asked, but her heart was still her own.

Brenna grabbed Bianca's arm. "I think we need some air. Excuse us, sirs." She dragged her sister across the room, toward the stairs.

Vasco took a step away from the table, intending to follow the princesses.

"So will she do it?" Brenna's prince asked Corbin.

"By the time I am done seducing her, of course she will," Corbin said easily, pouring himself some wine. "She'll make a sweet wife, that one. I'll enjoy the wedding night."

The other prince laughed. "I wager Fiachra won't. He will not forgive you for foisting the slave's daughter on him while you kept the jewel for yourself."

Corbin drained his cup. "You know, you might be

right, Raban. I know we only need them for one night to break the curse, but I might just keep that one. She'd make a fine mistress of Beacon Isle."

Raban laughed even harder. "I'll wager you tire of her in a week, or you'll give her to Fiachra to silence his complaints. By the time we reach Beacon Isle, we'll have all had her so many times she won't be able to close her legs. She won't be fit for a whorehouse, let alone our father's house."

Corbin shrugged. "Mayhap you're right. Who cares? The curse will be broken, and there are more women in the world than we could bed in a lifetime." He reached for Bianca's goblet, which she'd left on the table, and downed the contents. Wiping his mouth with the back of his hand, he added, "But the next woman I bed will be that one. Tomorrow, if I am any judge. Come, let's go find them. I must have her answer."

Let it be no, Vasco prayed. Bianca deserved better. A prince he might be, but he and his brothers were kin to toads, not kings, if they thought to treat her that way. She was far too precious to be thrown away on such men who were so far beneath her they did not deserve to even look at her.

He snatched up the empty goblet and tucked it under his cloak with the tree branch. This would end tonight.

Vasco marched through the dancers, taking the stairs two at a time in his hurry to leave. Choosing the nearest boat, he jumped in and poled himself back through the mists to shore. Dawn was whispering her way into the sky already, but the sun wasn't up yet.

When he reached the beach, he leaped onto the sand and shoved the boat back out onto the lake. If he was lucky, the princes would assume it had drifted away on its own.

Only when he was outside the palace proper did he remove his cloak, using it to wrap the goblet and branch as he strode to the Lord Steward's chambers. He had solved the mystery of the princesses' shoes, and it was far more sinister than he'd thought.

Twenty-Nine

Brenna didn't release Bianca's arm until they'd reached the surface. "What are you thinking?" Brenna hissed.

Bianca folded her arms across her chest. "I'm thinking of my future. I don't know that man!"

"Who cares? Do you think our father would let you get to know a man if he promised you in marriage?"

Still Bianca didn't budge. "If he intended to use us to forge a marriage alliance, we wouldn't be here. We'd be in the women's palace still, under the queen's watchful eyes. He sent us here to become spinsters. He will never let us marry."

"So take your life in your own hands! Now you have a chance to make your own choices. To marry, have children. Don't you want children?" Brenna demanded. "Or do you want to have a succession of dogs that die too soon?" She swiped at her tears.

"I'm sorry about your dog, Brenna, and yes, I would like to marry and have children," Bianca said carefully. "But..."

But...what? Corbin was everything a prince should be. Charming, courteous...handsome, even. She could do worse.

"You have known the freedom of the Summer Palace for many months. I have scarcely tasted it in my few weeks here. Why, this is my first night dancing with all of you. I would like a little more time," she finished.

Brenna closed her eyes. "I understand. Truly, I do. But you must understand that there is far more at stake. At any time, our father might recall one of us back to the palace, to marry the man he chooses. And the princes themselves...they are cursed, and they suffer so. They are confined to these chambers during daylight hours, only venturing out at night under the light of the moon. They need our help to break the curse. All of our help. There are a dozen princes, and twelve of us. In order to break the curse, they must each find a maiden willing to pledge her love and life to them. All at the same time. Only then will they be free."

Bianca couldn't seem to close her mouth. "Why didn't you tell me this earlier?" she demanded. "The princes are prisoners? Who would do such a thing?"

Brenna shook her head. "A wicked witch cursed them for some imagined slight. She did not bother to tell them her name. But we can release them, sister. And take them as husbands. Princes — our father cannot object when we marry princes! Tell me you will accept his offer, Bianca. All of our futures depend on it."

Bianca turned away, not wanting Brenna to see how torn she was. On the one hand sat Corbin and his brothers, trapped by a terrible curse that she alone had the power to free them from. Yet on the other hand stood Vasco, who would die if he did not share the secret of the princes with Cousin Efe.

She bowed her head. "Very well. I shall marry Prince Corbin."

"Did you hear that? She says yes!"

Bianca whirled to find Corbin and one of his brothers only a few yards away. She and Brenna were led back into the ballroom, where Corbin announced what he'd overheard to everyone, prince and princess alike.

A rousing cheer erupted, and Bianca began to believe she had made the right choice. What was one man's life compared to the fate of a dozen men, not to mention her sisters?

"Tomorrow, we will be wed. What say you?" Corbin boomed.

More cheering, drowning out Bianca's surprised exclamation. Tomorrow? She would marry the man tomorrow?

She swallowed. Why wait? If she had made her choice, there was no sense in delaying the inevitable. Summoning a watery smile, she joined in the celebration.

Thirty

"…And that's how the girls dance their shoes to pieces every night," Vasco finished triumphantly.

The Lord Steward continued to stroke the golden goblet. "So let me get this straight. They have a secret trapdoor in their bedchamber, which is how they escape to the lake where a pack of ruffians claiming to be princes carry them to a secret underground ballroom where they dance all night until their shoes are destroyed. Then the ruffians bring them back, so the girls can get some sleep and new shoes before doing it all again the following night."

Vasco nodded. "I think they mean to carry them off, but they haven't yet. I heard two of them talking, but I didn't hear enough to be certain."

The Lord Steward rose, setting the cup on his desk. "Very good, soldier. You have earned a reward. I shall send these with a note to the king this very morning. I will have a flagon of my best wine sent up to help you sleep, for I am sure you need rest."

Vasco tried and failed to smother a yawn. "Yes." He gave a perfunctory bow and left the Lord Steward's chambers. He limped all the way up to his pallet and struggled to remove his boots so he could sleep.

Gentle laughter made him look up. Gerel stood in the princesses' audience chamber, holding what Vasco presumed was the promised flagon. "I can help you, if you wish."

Vasco grunted and with one final effort managed to pull off one boot. The other took even longer.

He stared longingly at the flagon. "What's in it?"

Gerel set his boots neatly side by side at the end of his bed, then smoothed the folds of his cloak as she hung it on its customary hook. "Wine from the hogshead you were so interested in yesterday morning."

Vasco had almost managed to lie down, but he shot up again. "The one with the crow?"

Gerel wrinkled her nose. "The one with a bowl of dead rats in front of it."

Vasco swore, then apologised. "Why did you draw

the wine from that cask, and not one of the others?"

"Lord Steward's orders. Otherwise, I would've chosen any cask but the one with the rats."

Absently, he thanked her and dismissed her.

Did the Lord Steward know it was poisoned? And if he did, why would he want to poison Vasco, after he'd finally solved the mystery?

Movement outside caught his eye. Vasco crept to the window, peering out carefully so that he could see without being seen.

On the beach, he saw the Lord Steward standing by the water's edge. He drew something out of his pocket that glinted in the morning sun, then pitched it into the lake. The golden goblet flew in a glittering arc for a moment before it plopped into the depths.

All thoughts of sleep fled. The Lord Steward wasn't sending anything to the king. Instead, he'd destroyed the evidence Vasco brought him and tried to poison him. Did he want the girls to be carried off by these mysterious princes to dishonour and who knew what else?

Well, Vasco wouldn't let them. He might not be a prince or even a lord, but he knew where his duty lay. He had to protect the princesses, even if it cost him his life. Except...he didn't know how he could possibly do that now.

He needed someone who understood intrigues and

politics to tell him what to do. So he did the only thing he could think of.

It was time to ask Princess Bianca for help.

Thirty-One

It felt like Bianca's head had barely touched the pillow before she was awake again. Someone was calling her name.

"Mm?" she said, hoping this was a dream.

"Princess Bianca, I'm sorry to wake you, but I need your help. Mistress Kun told me if I ran into trouble, I must ask you. Please, Princess Bianca." Vasco's voice was far too earnest for this to be a dream.

"Give me a moment to dress. I shall meet you outside," she mumbled, prying her eyes open. The light streaming through the open door told her it was dawn. Ugh. She shouldn't have drunk so much wine last night. Surely it had only been two cups. Perhaps three. Surely not four or five. Her sisters had drunk more, she was certain of it. They would sleep for hours yet, while she had a promise to Kun to keep.

The moment her feet touched the floor, she regretted it. Her head ached, but it was nothing to the tenderness of her feet. Dancing all night, dancing so much she wore through the soles of her shoes, was not something she ever wanted to do again. She'd taken her ruined shoes off in the boat, letting her feet soak in the surprisingly warm lake water, but the walk up to the palace from the lake had been tortuous. The path had been littered with so many sharp rocks she feared her feet had been cut to ribbons. She would not be dancing tonight, that was for certain.

Shielding her eyes from the far too bright light in the audience chamber, she could barely make out Vasco, silhouetted against the window. "What is it?"

"I followed you last night. I now know the answer to how you and your sisters dance your shoes to pieces every night," he said gravely.

Good, she thought muzzily. Then she had no need to venture to the island or dance until dawn ever again.

"I brought back some items from the island, and showed them to the Lord Steward when I told him my story."

Bianca nodded, then winced as the movement only made her head ache more. She'd wager Cousin Efe had been shocked by Vasco's discovery. Now he could claim the palace and his bride and…

Bride. Her memories of last night threw up an image she'd forgotten until now. Tonight, there would be a wedding in the underwater ballroom. Someone called Corbin was going to be married, or was it one of her sisters? More than one, maybe. Bianca wished it weren't so foggy in her head. There'd been much celebration and cheering, hence the wine, and…

"He promised to send the evidence with a note to the king, then gave me a flagon of wine, before he threw all my evidence in the lake. It was poisoned wine. The Lord Steward doesn't want the mystery solved. He wants me dead, and you and your sisters carried off to dishonour. I need your help to stop him."

Vasco's words started to sink in, and Bianca stared at him. Surely she hadn't heard right. "You think Cousin Efe is a traitor, who would deliberately withhold information from my father, the king?"

Vasco looked scared. "Perhaps. That is why I need your help. If the Lord Steward is not to be trusted, the king will never know I solved his mystery, and you will be…those princes have plans for you and your sisters, princess. They mean to use you to break some sort of curse, but they will discard you the moment the spell is broken."

"I know about the curse," she said absently. She did. She couldn't remember what she knew about it, but it certainly sounded familiar. It didn't matter, though. What mattered was saving Vasco's life. Vasco shouldn't die if he'd solved the mystery. He should present his case to the king in person. "You must tell the king what you know."

Vasco laughed mirthlessly. "The king will not listen to a common soldier."

Bianca knew he was right. Her father was a busy man.

"Then we must return to the island on the lake and gather as much proof as we can." Bianca surprised herself by the vehemence in her tone.

"Thank you, princess. I will find us a boat." Vasco sketched a hasty bow and hurried away.

"And I will find the kitchens, and some willow bark tea," she muttered to herself, vowing never to drink wine again.

<h1 style="text-align:center">Thirty-Two</h1>

Vasco asked a manservant whose name he did not know where he might find a boat.

"There is a whole fleet of pleasure boats in the boatshed, usually," the man said, pointing. "But the Lord Steward went out on the lake this morning. The boat he used should still be on the beach, as he hasn't asked me to put it away yet."

Vasco thanked the man, offering to return the boat to the boatshed when he was finished with it. That way, no one would know when he and Bianca returned from their errand — or see what evidence they carried. Vasco trusted no one now, except perhaps Gerel. Bianca…that remained to be seen.

He paused by the kitchen to ask for a basket of provisions for the day. Gerel smiled broadly when she heard him ask for food and drink for two, but she didn't ask questions. Perhaps she already knew his partner in the day's activities would be Princess Bianca, and she fancied some sort of romance between the two of them. Vasco suppressed a snort. As though a princess would stoop so low as to fall in love with a soldier. He should be thankful she had agreed to help him at all.

Her life depended on the outcome of today's expedition just as much as his did. He couldn't forget that. Still, that didn't mean she needed to put herself in danger. He could easily go to the island and return while she stayed in the safety of the palace. More than anything, he wanted to protect her.

Lifting his chin and straightening his spine, he marched to the dining hall to tell her what he'd decided.

"You should have some breakfast, Vasco," she greeted him, gesturing for him to sit down.

Obediently, he sat, and reached for some fruit. "I've been thinking, and it seems to me that it is too dangerous for a princess to be haring about across the lake. You should stay here, where you will be safe."

"Where the Lord Steward is cousin to the queen, a woman who likes me so little she exiled me out here?

To a man who poisons people." She sipped from her cup and set it down. "It seems to me that I will be safer outside the palace than in it."

"But – " he began.

She interrupted, "Last night seems like little more than a fever dream, with boats in the mist, charming fairy princes, and dancing until dawn. I need to see where it all happened in daylight, to know I did not dream it. I need the evidence of my eyes as much as you want items you can take to prove what you have seen."

"But Princess Bianca…"

She waved him into silence. "If we are to sneak around the island, I cannot be a princess today. I am merely Bee, as my mother liked to call me. Buzzing around, butting my head into matters that do not concern me. Though today, they most certainly do concern me."

Curiosity got the better of him. "What does your father call you?"

Bianca sighed heavily. "I do not know. I'm not sure my father even knows my name. He has so many children, so many daughters, that I am just one in a multitude." She flashed a rueful smile. "So while you call me princess, the pampered daughter of a king, which I am, were anything to happen to me…I'm not sure my father would know, or even care."

"I would know, and I would care a great deal," Vasco said gravely.

"Truly?"

He nodded. "I have no right to give you orders, though I wish you would stay here. But if you will not…then it is my duty to go with you and protect you."

She drained her cup and set it on the table. "I'm ready when you are. You might want your cloak, though." Bianca winked. "It might be helpful for sneaking around."

It sounded almost as though she knew its magical properties. Had Kun told her? Or had she glimpsed him last night and said nothing?

"As you wish," he said. He rose, bowed, and went to retrieve his cloak.

Thirty-Three

Bianca caught Vasco stealing glances at her last night when she wore the ornate silk dress her sisters had insisted upon, but today he'd gone back to not meeting her eyes again. As though he fancied himself a servant, and not the rightful lord of the Summer Palace. Which he was, now, by her father's own conditions. Never mind that Cousin Efe had rejected his claim to have solved the mystery – Bianca knew he had.

Even the drab clothes she'd donned today did little to dispel his servility. Sure, she was a princess, but she was a woman first. Last night, he'd looked like he recognised that. Now, she wasn't so certain. Still, if he called her Bee, just the once…

He took her down to the beach that last night had been littered with lantern-lit pleasure boats, but now only held one aging boat in need of fresh paint, which had oars instead of a pole. Unlike the pleasure boats, this one could have held at least half a dozen people comfortably – maybe more if they were as slim as her sisters.

He said little as he rowed out to the island, except to comment on the absence of last night's mist.

That meant that anyone could see them on the lake. Bianca felt the hair rise on the back of her neck, as though hostile eyes watched her.

"Put on the cloak," she ordered.

"There is no point. It won't cover the boat," he said, rowing steadily.

"Put it on anyway," she insisted, biting her lip as she started to cast a spell that would hide the boat from sight as well.

"If you sit here beside me, it will cover us both," he said.

Bianca considered telling him she was quite capable of taking care of herself, thank you, but something in the way he held out his arm, ready to pull her to his side, melted something inside of her. Instead she said, "Thank you," and carefully shifted to the bench beside him.

The prickling sensation was gone almost instantly,

replaced with the warm presence of the man beside her. She could feel the hardness of his muscles as he rowed, the lulling sensation as they contracted and relaxed around her. His chest, his arm…oh, it was everything she'd imagined as she watched him work on Kun's house.

When her father asked Vasco to choose one of his daughters to be his bride, Bianca wanted it to be her.

The boat grated on sand, jolting her out of her fantasies.

"We're here," Vasco said.

He helped her out of the boat and they both stood on the shore, surveying the island.

"What sort of evidence did you give to Efe?" Bianca asked.

"I broke off a branch from one of the trees. They only grow here on this island." Vasco stepped forward and seized a branch. This time, he tossed it into the boat, then threw several more on top of it. "I also had a goblet from the banquet table in the ballroom."

"But we can't go into the ballroom. That's where the princes will be. They won't help us," Bianca said, then stopped. How did she know that?

Vasco didn't question her knowledge, though. He merely nodded and said, "So we sneak in under my cloak?"

Would invisibility be enough? Bianca had to hope

so. After all, no one but she had seen Vasco last night. She nodded.

At the top of the hill, Bianca stood back while Vasco raised the trapdoor.

The spiral staircase disappeared into the darkness. "I'll go first," Vasco said. "You keep close behind me, and stay under the cloak as much as you can."

If she hadn't been fighting the rising dread of what awaited her in the underground chamber, Bianca might have refused. As it was, she wrapped one arm around his waist and slipped under the woollen folds. Vasco was a comforting bulk in front of her as they made their way slowly down the steps.

"There's no one here," Vasco whispered.

Even in the darkness, Bianca could see that he was right. The antechamber where they'd left their cloaks last night was empty. Yet light shimmered at the end of the passage, tempting her to enter.

"No goblets, either," she whispered back.

That was enough to impel him forward. What could Bianca do but follow?

Together, they shuffled along the passage to the ballroom.

She heard his gasp as he stepped out of the passage, but she couldn't see past his bulk to work out what had elicited such a response. Before she could struggle free of his cloak, he let it slide off his shoulders, and draped it over his arm.

"The whole place is empty. There's no one here. No princes, nothing. Just the remains of last night's revelry," he said.

"What startled you, then?" she asked.

"There are no torches, yet it's as bright in here as it was last night. Look up, princess." Vasco caught her around the waist and pointed up.

Bianca lifted her eyes to the ceiling and it was her turn to gasp. Last night's moonlight was nothing to the sun filtering through the water now. Shades of blue and green, even rainbows, shimmered across the glass.

"It's beautiful," she breathed.

"Not as beautiful as…never mind," he muttered, half under his breath. The arm around her middle released her.

"You've seen a place more beautiful than this?" Bianca asked. "It must be a great thing, to have travelled and seen so much."

Vasco chuckled. The sound echoed strangely around the underground room. "I was thinking of you. You looked beautiful last night. The perfect marriage of summer sky and moonlight."

She stared at him, and for the first time today, he met her gaze. He seemed a little embarrassed by his admission, but the look in his eyes was honest. Unlike all the other fools with their empty compliments, he truly meant his.

And if she didn't tear her gaze away from his, she was going to throw her arms around his neck and kiss him until she couldn't breathe.

Bianca closed her eyes. "Summer sky and moonlight. I wish I could be as free as both of those things. I might even dance…"

Another chuckle. "I bet your prince from last night has sore feet this morning. I lost count of the number of times you stepped on his feet while you were dancing."

Perhaps his honesty wasn't quite as attractive as she'd first thought. It certainly broke the spell between them, allowing Bianca to seize two of the goblets from the table. "Here. These should replace the one you gave to Efe."

Vasco tucked them in a fold of his cloak. "Thank you. Now we have what we came for, shall we head back to shore?"

Bianca wanted to say yes, for this beautiful place frightened her more than she was willing to admit. Yet she was so certain the princes would be here. They couldn't leave the island, she was sure, because of something half-remembered that she'd heard last night. Something about the curse. "We should finish exploring the island. The princes must be here, and the food and wine has to come from somewhere."

"As you wish." Vasco led the way back to the surface.

The hilltop clearing where the trapdoor lay had only the one path leading off it – the one which led back to the boat, so they followed that to the beach and trudged through the sand, looking for signs of another path.

The beach ended in a collection of tumbled rocks before they were a quarter of the way around the island. Vasco helped her climb up the slope. Bianca wasn't sure whether it was a path or simply the fact that nothing grew on the bare rock, but she glimpsed another beach through the rocks. Without waiting for Vasco, she trudged on until she stood on a cliff overlooking a beach like nothing she'd ever seen before.

The sand was black, with occasional pieces of bleached wood scattered along it. Then something moved, exposing a flash of pink and red, before it was hidden from sight once more. One flash was enough.

Bianca blinked, her mouth falling open in horror. Deep within her, she felt a scream fighting to escape.

Thirty-Four

When Vasco reached Bianca's side, it was already too late to stop her from seeing the horror no one should ever be subjected to. The corpse-strewn beach had bodies in various states of decay, from scattered bones to a cadaver so fresh the flesh the crows ripped off it was still red and moist. No, not crows — ravens, he corrected himself. He counted a dozen of them picking at the corpse, which still wore the tatters of clothing in a particularly brilliant shade of pink.

He knew the expression on her face all too well. Every soldier viewing a battlefield for the first time looked like that. But she was no soldier. Why, the princess had probably never seen blood that was not her own until today.

"Princess," he whispered.

No response. Her mouth gaped, but no sound came out.

He prayed she would forgive him for the liberty. "Bee. Look away."

She blinked. Once. Twice. Then she turned and flung herself into his arms, pressing her face against his chest. Sobs shook her body. "No. All those men."

He eyed the pink-clad body. "Women, too, I think. One of them wore pink silk."

Bianca shook her head violently. "No. I remember that tunic. The foolish adventurer who came before you wore that. He's dead, Vasco. Dead because my sisters wanted to go dancing! And if we do not stop it, you will be next!"

"I should have died when the rest of my village was slaughtered. Yet here I stand. We all must die sometime." The words slipped out before he could stop them.

She squinted up at him. "How can you be so calm? There are dead bodies on that beach. Have you killed so many people that you no longer care when someone dies?"

Vasco sighed. "I do care. In my dreams, I see the faces of everyone I knew who has died, while I yet live. Every enemy soldier I have killed. Every brother in arms who died at my side when an enemy sword took them instead of me. Every man, woman and child in my village, whose bodies burned with the village itself. Eudokia…my Dokia…who agreed to meet me one evening by the river. We were betrothed, but the wedding could not come soon enough for us, and there was no privacy in the village. A scouting party found us, too engrossed in each other to notice the men until they were upon us. One knocked me out, and the others…" Vasco swallowed, blinking back tears. "They left me for dead, and when I woke, they had thrown her body atop mine. She was naked, and they had done unspeakable things to her before they killed her while I lay senseless and useless. I should have saved her."

Bianca clapped a hand to her mouth. "Ancestors, I am so sorry! That poor girl. What did you do then?"

"I took what little was left in the village of value, and traded it for arms and equipment when I joined the army. I trained hard and vowed to fight for those who still had their homes and their families, because I could not fight for my own. I became a soldier, living only for vengeance, until one day that was not enough. That day, I took an arrow in the knee that dwells there still." He shook his head. "I should not have let you see this. No woman should see this. Dokia's spirit would never forgive me if I let you and your sisters join this graveyard. I will do anything I have to in order to save you from this fate."

As though the creature had heard him, one of the ravens lifted its head and fixed a beady eye on Vasco. The creature appeared to have a band of greyish feathers around its head, like a kind of crown. It made a menacing sound low in its throat. The other birds looked up from their meal, their beaks still red with gore. As one, they turned to stare at Vasco. The menace emanating from them was unmistakeable.

"Bianca…" he said softly. "Princess, we need to go."

One of the birds extended its wings and started to run toward them.

"Now." Vasco threw his cloak around his shoulders, scooped her up in his arms, and ran. "Fasten the cloak," he urged her. "Then they won't be able to see us."

The first bird had made it into the air, and it took advantage of its height to dive at them. Vasco felt claws scrabble at his hood, but they didn't seem to be able to grab a hold of it.

Bianca's pale arm rose up, her hand clenched into a fist, and she punched the raven. The bird squawked and fell away, but not without raking its claws over her hand.

She didn't cry out. Instead, she brought her

bleeding finger to her mouth. "Get us to the boat. I'll take care of the birds."

Vasco didn't have the breath to argue. His wounded leg screamed at him, but nothing mattered more than keeping Bianca safe.

He set her down on the bench, wrapped his cloak around her, and shoved the boat away from the beach. He jumped in, taking a seat on the bench beside her, and plied the oars.

Only when they reached open water did she seem to recover a little. She arranged the cloak over them both, tucking herself against his side. "The boat might be visible, but they won't see us," she said with quiet confidence.

Vasco scanned the sky, but he couldn't see the birds any more. "I think they're gone."

"Not gone. They just can't find us while we travel unseen. Did you see the crowns on their heads?" She sounded so calm.

"You mean the light coloured feathers?"

"Crowns," she corrected. "Each one was slightly different. Just like the ones the princes wore last night. And there were twelve of them. Dark magic clings to them like mist. Those were not normal birds."

"Ravens are meant to be very intelligent. I have heard tales of wise men who kept them as pets. Perhaps your princes do the same." Vasco didn't believe a word of it. Those ravens were on the beach for the carrion feast spread across the black sand.

"Those birds are not pets," she said. "They knew you would be their next meal." She swallowed. "Vasco, what if those birds are the princes? Carrion crows by day, and charming men by night? My sisters…my sisters are in danger. You must go to the king and tell him. Tell him what you have found. Cursed princes trying to seduce his daughters to their deaths. Take the ring from my finger, and take my horse. Ride to the capital. You must." She swallowed again, fighting to keep her eyes open. "I will warn my sisters and try to keep them away from the island. You must tell my father."

Vasco glanced down. She slumped against him. Asleep or unconscious, he wasn't sure, but it mattered little. However crazy her thoughts sounded, they tallied with his own. He must ride for the capital, trusting no one but the king himself. For Bianca, he would do anything.

He rowed the boat to the boatshed, where he dragged it out of the water. In the shadows, he saw the shapes of many small boats – the pleasure boats they'd used last night. The princes used the palace's own boats! Then that meant…

The Lord Steward truly was in league with them.

"Princess, you must wake. I can't leave you here

with him. Not if he is at the heart of this," Vasco said, but Bianca's eyes stayed shut. Frustrated, he lifted her in his arms and carried her up to the house. She did not even wake when he laid her on her own bed, and pulled off her boots. He didn't dare remove anything else.

He watched her for a moment, but there was nothing he could do here. It would be a long, hard ride to the capital – and it would take much longer if he carried the unconscious princess with him. He must go now, alone, for it was the fastest way to save her from the clutches of the Lord Steward and his pet ravens, or princes, or whatever they were. Demons, surely.

"Stay safe, princess, and don't leave this room until I return," he whispered. Planting a quick kiss on her forehead, he turned and strode out of the room.

Thirty-Five

"You can't go dancing tonight," Bianca insisted for what felt like the hundredth time. Her head had started to ache again, but this was too important to wait. When they listened to her, then she could ask the kitchen for some more willow tea to ease the pain.

"Of course we can, and we will," Brenna said smoothly. "Don't be silly. Tonight is too important to miss. Tonight, we shall be free." Her face glowed. "Do you think I should wear the white or the pink?" She held up both gowns.

Bianca shuddered. White bones and pink silk, as the raven princes pecked at a bloody corpse that had once been a man. "Neither. Don't you see? They will kill us and strip the flesh from our bones!"

"Who will?" Melania asked.

"The cursed princes, of course! By night, they look like handsome men, but in truth, they are carrion crows. I have seen them!" Bianca said.

Hazel patted her shoulder. "Just a dream, sister. You went to bed when we did, just before dawn, and I shook you awake myself not an hour ago. Whatever you thought you saw, it was a nightmare brought on by too much wine and excitement. Do not drink so much tonight, for you will not want to alarm your new husband on your wedding night."

The thought of a wedding night with Vasco sent blood rushing to Bianca's cheeks. But that would not be tonight, surely. He hadn't returned from the capital yet, but he should be there by now. Hopefully telling her father all about the princes and Efe. If all went well, he would return by this time tomorrow, and he'd choose her for his bride, surely. He'd barely noticed the other girls, but he'd watched her so closely he knew she'd stepped on Corbin's feet when they danced.

Corbin…wedding…Bianca's memory itched, but she'd had too little sleep to understand what it was trying to tell her.

"What dress are you wearing tonight?" Hazel asked, opening the chest that contained Bianca's clothes.

"That blue you wore last night was so lovely."

"Black," Bianca said absently. What other colour could she wear when her thoughts were as dark as ravens' wings?

"Ooh, I love the embroidery on this one. You should wear your hair loose tonight, cascading over it," Hazel gushed, helping Bianca into the black gown. Her mother had embroidered it with fish in silver thread which seemed to move if they caught the light right. "Corbin won't be able to take his eyes off you."

Bianca didn't care what Corbin did. He wouldn't see her, because… "I'm not going," she said flatly.

Brenna stormed across the room and slapped Bianca's face hard. "What is wrong with you? Stop this madness!"

Bianca rubbed her cheek and glared back. "What is wrong with you? Don't you hear what I'm saying? The princes are cursed!"

"I told you about the curse last night," Brenna returned. "And how it could be broken, which is when you agreed to become Corbin's wife while the rest of us marry his brothers. Together, we will break the curse and we will all be free!"

"We will be dead!" Bianca insisted.

Brenna raised her hand to slap her again, but Bianca caught it this time before the blow could land.

"You're a fool if you think the princes have any

love for us. They only want us to break the curse, and after that, we are expendable. You'll see," Bianca said. "I'll go with you to the island tonight. And I'll show you what they truly are."

"Princes who want to marry us!" Nera giggled.

Bianca gave up. While her sisters busied themselves about their toilette, she opened the trapdoor and headed down to the beach. She left her torch in a bracket at the bottom of the stairs, preferring to use just the moonlight to make her way to the lake. There was no need to pretend to stumble so that Vasco could catch up tonight – he had all the proof he needed.

The fog hadn't engulfed the lake yet, so when she heard a commotion by the boathouse, she could clearly see the little pleasure boats making their way out of it.

"You fool! You nearly capsized me. For that, you, Ronne and Guntram can take the food to the island. Set it up as quickly as you can, and hurry back. Our brides will be here soon, and everything must be perfect!"

Bianca recognised Corbin's voice from the previous night, but it hadn't sounded so imperious then. Was he the eldest of the raven princes? Had he led the attack against them this morning? Her blood froze in her veins at the thought that she'd let him touch her. A carrion-pecking crow. She would not allow him the same liberty tonight. The moment she reached the island, she would take her sisters to the cove full of corpses and show them the princes' handiwork. They might not believe her words, but they would believe their eyes. *Better to see a corpse than to become one before your time*, she thought grimly.

She hid behind a rock as the boats sailed past, headed for the island and the fog bank that only now crept over the lake, as if by some magical command. Yet there was no magic in it. If there was, she would sense it, she was sure of it.

The magic around the princes was there, though she'd been too busy to notice it last night. It was less noticeable on them when they were human – more concentrated when they were birds.

When the lake returned to its normal, glassy calm, showing no sign of the boats that had rippled its surface only moments before, Bianca heard the cheerful chatter of her sisters coming down the stairs to join her. If only they knew what awaited them tonight…but they hadn't listened, so they did not.

The boats arrived through the mist once more and they boarded them. Bianca managed to do so without Corbin's assistance, to her delight and his annoyance, though he smoothed his face back into a smile so quickly she almost doubted what she'd seen.

"You look so beautiful in that gown, it will be a pity to take it off for our wedding night," he said as he wrapped his hands around his pole and plied it vigorously. The boat set off so abruptly that a wave of water splashed over the side, soaking her shoes. "Forgive me, Bianca. I am so eager to make you mine that I forgot myself."

She suspected that it was more likely he'd forgotten anything but himself and his own desires, but she forced herself to smile and say nothing.

His eagerness got them across the lake in record time. By the time they'd reached the island, the others had only made it halfway.

Bianca climbed out of the boat before Corbin could offer his hand, and just as she was congratulating herself on managing to keep him from touching her, she felt his arms close around her waist like the cinch of a saddle.

He inhaled deeply as his lips grazed her throat. "By all that's holy, you're beautiful. I can scarcely wait to find out what you taste like."

Ravens with red-stained beaks, dripping gobbets of flesh. Bianca gave a delicate shudder. He would never taste her, alive or dead.

She twisted out of his grasp, bit down hard on her lip, and vanished from sight.

Thirty-Six

For what Vasco knew was the thirteenth time, though it wouldn't be the last, he said, "I already told you. I've come to speak to the king. He offered a reward for anyone who can solve the mystery of the shoes danced to pieces, and I have his answer."

But the guards at the palace laughed, taunted him, or bluntly told him they'd heard nothing about any such thing, and that he would never be granted entry to the palace, let alone the king's court.

Worse, Vasco knew how crazy he sounded. Were he a guard, he would probably behave much like these men were doing. But that didn't change the fact that Bianca was in danger, and he needed to speak to the king in order to keep her safe. Nothing else mattered.

Finally, he gusted a huge, sorrowful sigh and thanked the guards for their patience. He trudged across the courtyard and rounded a corner where he figured he'd be out of their line of sight. In a practiced motion, he swung his cloak around his shoulders and fastened it, before bring the hood up over his head. A moment passed and he could see through the thick wool as if it didn't exist, yet he knew he was invisible to everyone else. Kun had used powerful magic when she cast the invisibility spell on this cloak. He wished he'd had a second one to give Bianca to keep her safe from those raven princes.

As it was, he needed to hurry. Time was of the essence.

He strode past the guards, then a second set, and a third. Though he had never been to the capital before, the king's court was the subject of legend – everyone knew it was in the highest hall, in the very heart of the palace. So up he went, sweeping past anyone who might have stopped him if they could see him, until he stood at bottom of the steps to the very doors themselves.

Which swung shut before he could set his foot on the first step.

"There will be no further audience with the king today. If you have a petition, return tomorrow," a guard in a fancy uniform shouted to the crowd.

People grumbled and slowly dispersed.

Vasco hesitated for a moment, but the thought of Bianca spurred him on. The king was her father. It was his responsibility, nay, his duty to keep her safe. The king would see him. And if there was no audience, then there would be no one to interrupt him before he told his tale.

His knee was stiff from riding and walking so far, so he laboured up the steps like an old man. When he reached the top, he had to push against the doors with his whole weight, for they were heavier than he'd thought. The stories about the doors were true, then — they were made of solid gold, or at least solid metal, for no timber was that heavy.

"I told you, no more petitioners!" a man roared from the opposite end of the huge hall that was the king's court. A look of puzzlement crossed his face as he rose from his ornate throne. This man was the king, and Bianca's father.

Vasco continued until he reached the foot of the dais that held the king's throne. Only then did he fall to one knee as he whipped off his cloak. "Forgive me, your majesty, but your daughters are in great danger."

The king jumped a foot off the ground. Given the man was wearing enough metal to make armour for three men, that was quite a feat. "Where did you come from?"

"The Summer Palace, where your daughter, Princess Bianca, bade me give you this." Vasco held out the ring he'd pulled from her finger. "Your steward has made a deal with demons, who even now are trying to seduce your daughters so that they might kill and eat them."

These words started an uproar among the crowd of people who remained in what Vasco realised wasn't an empty court after all.

The king held up his hands for silence. "Silence! I will hear what this man has to say!" he roared. In a slightly quieter tone, he added, "Where are my daughters now?"

"The Summer Palace still, I hope, but if the demons have succeeded, then they are on an island in the middle of the lake beside the palace. There is an underground chamber beneath the lake where – "

The king cut him off. "We will leave for the Summer Palace at once. No demon will steal my daughters from me." He snapped his fingers. "Have every soldier in the capital assembled on the training grounds outside the city before the sun sets. Let it be known that the man who kills the most demons may choose one of my daughters as his bride!"

Vasco had a vision of himself slaughtering every one of those raven princes, before asking the king for

Bianca. He almost laughed at the vision.

"What is funny?" the king demanded. "Why do you smile so?"

Vasco lifted his gaze to meet that of the king. "No part of this is funny, your majesty. But the thought of killing demons to save your daughters brings a fierce joy to my breast that I cannot help but smile at. No demon can withstand the might you will bring to bear on them. They will be crushed, as they should be."

"Yes, they will," the king said darkly.

Thirty-Seven

"Princess? Bianca, where are you?" Corbin called.

Pressed against the trunk of the nearest tree, Bianca suppressed the urge to shout back that she was out of reach, so he would never touch her again. She had first discovered her magical talents when playing hide and seek with her sisters. If she stayed still and made no sound, they would never find her.

Other boats landed on the beach, spilling out their passengers.

"Where is Bianca?" Hazel asked.

"I don't know," Corbin said. "One moment she was in my arms, begging for a kiss, and the next…she was stolen from me. I saw a shadow and then she just…disappeared. Whoever took her, I will hunt him down and make him pay!"

Liar, Bianca thought furiously. Corbin hadn't seen any shadow. With a chill, she realised his anger wasn't directed at some imagined captor, but at her. If he caught her, he intended to make her pay.

Never.

"She can't have left the island," one of the other princes said reasonably. "If we spread out and search, we will find her, and whoever has taken her."

"I'll take the princesses to the ballroom, where they will be safe. No need to risk losing anyone else this night," another man said.

"No." This time the voice was female – Brenna's. She continued, "Our sister is missing. She knows us, and will answer our calls. We can help you search, so that she will be found faster. The sooner she is found, the sooner we will all be married."

Bianca wasn't sure whether Brenna or her other sisters knew about her magical abilities. Her mother had insisted she keep it a secret in the harem, but in a place where secrets were the highest form of currency, even the most carefully whispered confidence could be betrayed.

A brief argument ensued between Corbin and Brenna, but when the other girls weighed in, the princes were forced to concede.

They didn't want to lose all their brides. One was bad enough, but a dozen rebellious princesses spelled disaster for their plot. Bianca couldn't have planned this better if she'd tried. If only she had a plan at all.

"Fiachra, you search the ballroom. Cormac and Guntram, take the west thicket. Raban and Ronne…" Corbin divided them into six search parties that set off across the island. That left just him and Bianca on the beach.

"Where are you, princess?" he whispered. "I know you can't have gone far. You are dressed for a ball, not a walk in the woods. It will go easier if you show yourself. The longer I have to hunt for you, the worse it will be for you when I do find you. And I will. Of all my brothers, I have always been the best hunter. It is fitting that the curse that began with a hunt will end with the best one of all, for the sweetest quarry in the world is a woman."

He had done this before, Bianca realised in horror. The bleached bones on the beach…did some of them belong to women? Or did he mean he'd been cursed for hunting women in the woods for sport?

Not just him. His brothers, too. For they were all cursed, not just him.

She couldn't let him find her. She would die, as would all her sisters, and no one would ever know how it had happened. The princes could kill again, and again, and there would be no one to stop them.

Why hadn't her magic included fireballs or the ability to kill just by looking at someone? Then she could fight and defend her sisters, ending these wicked princes forever. Not hug trees and hide, which is all she could do with her invisibility.

If she weren't so clumsy, she might have moved to a better spot, but all it would take was one sound and Corbin would know where she was, invisible or not.

A shrill scream ripped through the air, before a second joined it.

Two of her sisters had found the black beach, Bianca guessed.

Corbin swore and dashed in the direction of the screams.

Bianca took her chance, climbing into the nearest boat. They were all drawn up on shore so close to one another that it was almost easy to move from one to the other without needing to touch the ground. Or leave footprints, which she knew would be her undoing. She chose a boat that was closest to the water, hemmed in by other vessels that the princes would have to climb over in order to reach her. That would take time, and hopefully allow her to get away if they found her. Not that she knew how to paddle a boat, but it hadn't looked that hard when Corbin did it. If only she could make the boat invisible the way she'd done with Vasco for a moment before she lost consciousness. Because it wasn't just the boat she had to make invisible. It was the boat and the surface of the water beneath it and…

"Take her down to the ballroom and make her drink some wine," one of the men said.

Bianca ducked low, so only her eyes were above the gunwale of the boat. One of the princes tramped past, carrying a woman in his arms. She thought it might be Aruna, who'd been wearing a golden dress. He was followed by another pair. Nera's eyes stared at nothing as she walked like a woman in a dream. The prince beside her gripped her arm, tugging her along like she was a dawdling child.

Bianca ached to help them, but if she revealed herself, there was little she could do. No, her strength lay in hiding. If she could hide until dawn, the princes would turn back into birds and then she could help her sisters escape. Until then…she had to stay concealed.

Bianca settled in the bottom of the boat, out of sight even if she wasn't invisible. She liked the way the waves lapped at the boat, rocking it. So soothing. One day, when all this was over, she'd like to sleep in a boat. She'd heard of an ancient queen who had a pleasure barge that she sailed up and down the river. Bianca didn't need a whole barge. Just a boat big enough for her to lie down in. Just let it drift…

"She's escaping in the boat!"

Jolted from sleep, Bianca sat up. How had she fallen asleep? She stretched, knowing the stiffness in her limbs and the lightening sky meant she'd slept for several hours. And while she'd slumbered, as if responding to her unspoken command, the boat had drifted away from the shore with her in it. Now, she floated halfway between the island and the shore. That meant only half the distance to pole, she thought to herself, searching for the long paddle she'd seen the princes use.

Only…it wasn't in the boat. No pole or paddle or anything. Just the empty boat with her in it, while the princes had all the others at their disposal. They would catch up to her in minutes, drag her back to the island, and force her to marry that hateful man.

Bianca peered at the island. Through the mist, she couldn't tell if they were following her or not. It looked like the boats were still pulled up on shore.

The sun peeked above the horizon, blinding her as it turned the mist into blazing gold.

Then out of the mist flew a murder of crows.

Thirty-Eight

The king maintained a slow but steady pace that drove Vasco mad. Every moment, Bianca could be in more danger, yet the king seemed to be in no hurry. More than once, Vasco found himself drifting off to sleep, but he knew he could not. Bianca depended on him to bring help, and he would. He rode with an army at his back and her father, the king…well, he didn't ride precisely at his side, for the king's personal guard surrounded him, but Vasco was still close.

Finally, Vasco started to recognise the trees along the way. He knew they were near the Summer Palace when they passed Kun's cottage. Night was draining away, as the predawn light began to illuminate their path. One by one, they extinguished their torches, but still they rode. There would be no stopping until they reached the Summer Palace and saved the princesses.

What the king would say when he saw the demons were merely ravens, Vasco did not know, but nor did he care. The king could do whatever he liked with him, as long as Bianca was safe.

The Summer Palace loomed into view, a shadow between them and the lake.

"Summon the Lord Steward," the king commanded. A squad of soldiers dismounted and marched toward the door.

Vasco shook his head. The Lord Steward didn't matter. It was the princes who were the problem. "They will be on the lake," he said, directing his horse on a different path that led to the beach, or so he thought. Instead, he emerged beside the deserted archery range.

A single boat drifted into view, ominously empty.

Vasco heard shouts, but he wasn't sure whether they came from the island or the army behind him. He didn't care.

A chill breeze rippled the water of the lake, sending the boat in a lazy circle.

Shivering, Vasco pulled his cloak around him.

He glimpsed movement and then, a figure rose from the boat. Though he could only see her head and shoulders, he would know Bianca's pale hair anywhere. She was alive and unharmed. He was not too late.

Dawn kissed the horizon, setting her hair ablaze and turning the mist behind her into a glorious halo.

Yet in the light, there were shadows. First one, then two, then a dozen crows came flying out of the mist, arrowing straight for her.

No.

Vasco reached for his bow and strung it like a man in a dream. Nock, draw, aim, loose, the wind seemed to whisper, and he obeyed, like the good soldier he was.

"That's impossible!"

"It must be five hundred feet!"

"No one can shoot that far."

"Why is he shooting birds on an empty boat?"

Vasco paid no heed to the men behind him. His first arrow hit its target, a bird extending its talons toward Bianca's face. The bird flipped over and over before landing in the water with a splash.

All at once, a great wind ruffled the water, making it rise up in waves that carried the boat away from the stricken bird.

The ravens converged on their injured fellow, hiding it from sight for a moment before they rose up in one flock, flying over the lake and away across the forest. The body of the bird Vasco had shot had vanished.

Vasco paid no attention to the birds. His gaze was fixed on the boat making its way steadily to shore. It grounded on the bank just below him, and he ran to meet it, catching the edge of it so that the boat would not drift away again, no matter how the waves sucked at it.

Huddled in the bottom, her arms covered with cuts as they shielded her head, was Bianca.

Gently, Vasco reached for her, wrapping her in his cloak as he lifted her from the boat. "You're safe, princess," he murmured.

Bianca blinked. "Vasco?" She bit her lip, then seemed to shimmer like sun on the water.

"He has one of the princesses! She was hiding in the boat!" A great shout went up, carried by a multitude of throats.

"But where are the others?"

"Underground." Bianca cleared her throat, then tried again, louder this time. "They are in a chamber under the island. They needed all of us to break the curse. But they didn't get me. I'll show you where they are."

Vasco's arms tightened around her. "No. I will show them. You will stay here in the palace, safe under your father's care." There were few men he trusted, but the king was Bianca's father. If anyone could keep her safe, he could.

Reluctantly, he surrendered the woman he loved to her father, and set off to save her sisters.

Thirty-Nine

By the time the sun had burned away the mist, Bianca
stood with her sisters beside the archery range. No
other space was big enough to hold all of the warriors
the king had brought with him. She'd never seen so
many men in one place, but she had eyes only for one.
Vasco stood beside the king, looking as tired as she
felt, but none of that mattered. Sleep could wait, for
her future hung in the balance. Hers, and Vasco's.

Efe lay at her father's feet in chains, shouting about
liars and traitors and all manner of insults that Bianca
had never heard of, but they evidently offended
someone, because one of the men guarding him
pounded him with the butt of his spear until the

steward fell silent.

"You spoke of demons, but my men have found none. My steward says you imprisoned my daughters, but you insist upon blaming these demons. I will have the truth!" the king boomed.

Brenna stumbled forward. Her pink dress was smudged with black, as though she had fallen on the black beach. "The demons looked like men, claiming to be handsome princes who were our rightful bridegrooms, but they were beset by a terrible curse. By night, they danced and laughed and seduced us with lies. And by day…they turned into great black birds that ate corpses. I saw the bodies of those they had killed. And I saw with my own eyes as the sun rose…the men turned into birds and flew away."

"And what of this man?" The king pointed at Vasco.

Brenna shrugged. "He is some fool the Lord Steward employed to amuse us at dinner."

The king began to laugh. "A fool who sees true while my own daughters are foolish enough to fall for the lies told by demons?"

"Not all your daughters, sire. One fought them, and very nearly escaped, too." Vasco smiled at Bianca. "Perhaps I am a fool, but I was once a soldier. And I would defend your daughters with my life, even from demons."

"A soldier who shot one of the demons, too. Where is the monster's body?" the king asked.

"It seems the demons took the body with them when they left, your majesty," one of his personal guard said. "We saw the bird fall, but they gathered it up. Perhaps they are cannibals."

Bianca's stomach churned. She did not want to think of the princes' eating habits. She would have nightmares about blood-smeared beaks until the day she died.

Efe started shouting about liars and traitors and whores.

The king unsheathed his sword and set it at the bastard's throat. "You dare to call my daughters whores? You, a lying traitor who sold them to demons?"

A pained gurgle was the last sound Efe made before the king silenced him forever. Bianca turned her eyes away from the blood staining the sand. She had seen enough blood and death to last her a lifetime.

"So, after punishments, we come to rewards. It seems I owe you a reward, soldier. You saved my daughters' lives, yet the demons were allowed to escape. What will stop them from returning?" the king asked.

Vasco stepped forward. "I will. I shall set up camp on the island and should they ever return, I will slaughter them all."

"It seems to me there's a perfectly good house here. A fitting reward for a hero. I shall make you Lord of Raven Lake Estate, and you and your heirs will hold it against all enemies, demon or human," the king declared.

Vasco's mouth dropped open. Bianca almost laughed. Had he truly meant to camp on the island?

It was Bianca's turn to step forward. "That is not enough. He deserves more reward than just the house. He came to the Summer Palace to solve a mystery. You promised that anyone who could discover where the princesses went at night and danced their shoes to pieces might have both the house and a bride."

The king stared at her. Bianca knew she should bow her head, as any woman in his harem would, but she had endured too much from men tonight to bow to any of them.

"I made no such promise, and I have heard of no such mystery," he declared.

Bianca opened her mouth to protest.

"But I will honour it, all the same," the king continued. "Lord Vasco, in addition to this estate, you will need heirs to maintain the vigil when you are gone. For that, you will need a wife. I give you your choice of my daughters to be your bride."

Vasco's eyes met Bianca's, and it seemed like there

was no one else in the world but the two of them. She wished with all her might that he would choose her.

"I am but a soldier, though you honour me with more than I deserve," Vasco said carefully. "Your daughters are jewels indeed, worthy to be the brides of kings and princes. To them, I was but a fool at their table, not worthy of a princess for a wife, as I am sure they will tell you, if you but ask them. I will not marry a woman against her will."

The king glared at the girls. Several of them, already overcome by their ordeal, cringed away from his gaze.

Bianca stood firm. "I volunteer." She met her father's eyes once more. "He saved my life, and that of my sisters. I, Princess Bianca, would be honoured to be the wife of Lord Vasco." This time, she forced herself to drop a deep curtsey, first to her father, then to Vasco. "I've had my fill of princes and I will be happy never to meet another. Soldiers have far more honour than any prince."

Muffled laughter came from the assembled soldiers, which quickly died when the king held up his hands for silence.

"What do you say, Lord Vasco?" the king asked.

"The honour is mine," Vasco replied.

Bianca wasn't sure whose smile beamed brighter – hers, or Vasco's.

Forty

Vasco and Bianca were married that day, so the king could return home safely with his daughters. His guards kept a close watch on the traitorous steward, as if they thought his corpse might spring back to life again, and stuck him in a cart alongside the barrel of poisoned wine.

The girls huddled together in a second cart, barely saying a word, aside from a listless farewell to Bianca as their own cart rattled off down the road.

Leaving Bianca alone with her husband. A man she suddenly didn't know what to say to.

"Oh, good. I caught you before you dragged him off to bed," an elderly voice cackled.

Kun. Of all the things to say…Bianca felt her face grow red.

Vasco curled an arm around Bianca's waist and bowed to the old woman. "So you have heard our news, then. I couldn't have done this alone, and I will be forever grateful. You will be welcome in my home whenever you wish. Without your help – "

Kun laughed. "Without my help? You mean her help." She pointed a wrinkled finger at Bianca. "The invisibility cloak was her doing. She wanted answers, and she knew you stood a better chance of getting them than she could. After a few days of watching you work, she was itching to be your prize."

"My…prize?" Vasco stared at Bianca, before understanding dawned on his face. "So you truly did want to marry me? Not out of pity, or duty?" His eyes held so much hope.

No matter how brightly her face burned, Bianca forced herself to tell him the truth. "Every day you worked on Kun's house, I watched, invisible," she confessed. "Until one day when you were outside, I asked Kun to send you up to the palace to solve the mystery. I cast the spell on your cloak that rendered you invisible. I hoped that if I helped you, you might choose me." She frowned. "I had no idea that Kun didn't tell you that part of the reward."

Kun cackled. "It would have distracted him.

Thinking about his house and which girl he wanted for his wife. That's what killed the others. Distracted by a pretty girl who brings him a cup of wine, sending him dreaming of all the things he might do to her when they are married..." She flashed a gummy grin. "Oh, but I forgot. You two are married, and ready to do something about those dreams, I am sure. But humour an old lady for a moment. I have something to show you." She led them through the house to the room where the girls had once slept, now home to their discarded finery that would have to be sent up to the capital after them.

The trapdoor creaked open, moving without anyone touching the lever that normally worked the mechanism.

"How did you..." Bianca began, but Kun waved her into silence, beckoning them to follow her down the steps. Swallowing, Bianca did as she was bidden. It was daylight now, and there were no raven princes to attack or attempt to seduce her, but she couldn't suppress the thought that last night, she'd almost...

Vasco's arms wrapped reassuringly around her waist as if he could read her thoughts. "Don't you worry at all. If those accursed birds come anywhere near us again, I will pepper them so full of arrows, they'll look like they've grown a second set of feathers. I might not be accustomed to owning lands and being the lord responsible for them, but I have plenty of experience in defending them. I promised to keep you safe, Bianca, and I will."

She relaxed into his embrace, for she believed every word. And it felt good to be in his arms, his hard body pressed against hers, his breath on her neck…she wanted to turn around, take him back up the steps and do all the things married women did to the husband they loved. Maybe even let him do some things to her, too.

"I don't have all day!" Kun said. "You have all night to get naked, and the rest of your lives to work out what to do with each other. Can't an old lady ask for a few minutes of your time?"

Red-faced once more, Bianca continued down the steps with Vasco not far behind.

Kun led them down the path to the lake. Bianca didn't feel self-conscious at all as she grabbed Vasco's hand. After last night, she never wanted to walk this way alone. He squeezed her fingers gently and limped on at her side.

They reached the spot where Vasco had tripped that first night, almost giving himself away, and Kun stopped.

"This is it," she muttered, biting down on her lip. She waved her hands, an intense look of concentration on her face as she stared at the pile of rocks.

To Bianca's surprise, the topmost boulder rolled down, settling to the side of the road. The pile that had stretched higher than Bianca's head now arranged themselves in a rough ring. Around them, a small stream of water trickled, which had been hidden by the rocks before. As she watched, one of the tall, narrow stones toppled over, forming a natural drawbridge across the stream into the small fort.

Kun settled on a rock by the side of the path, a satisfied look on her face. "Go in and see."

When Bianca hesitated, Vasco stepped forward. A heartbeat later, she followed. Inside the stone circle was a pool, which was rapidly filling with water. Water that sent up wisps of mist or steam. Magic, surely.

"It's a hot spring," Kun said. "The earth has spots like this around, and if I'd left it alone, this one might have built enough pressure to blow some of the rocks off one day. Maybe not this week, but when your children take over the estate. Or their children. If you ever get around to having any."

"I have heard of places like this," Vasco said slowly. "They say the hot water works miracles. Healing old wounds, taking away stiffness and pain…"

"Yes," Kun said. "It relaxes you, too. Consider it a wedding present to the two of you." She bit her lip again. "Which reminds me…seeing as that new cloak was really a gift from your new bride, I still owe you a bonus for the service you did me." She bent over before Vasco and made a mysterious gesture with her hand beside his injured leg.

Vasco gave a cry of pain and Bianca's heart leapt into her throat. "What did you do to him?" Bianca demanded.

Kun turned her hand palm-up. Nestled among the wrinkles was a barbed arrowhead, glistening with blood. Vasco's blood, judging by the way he clutched at his knee. "I am no healer, for my talents lie with the earth. Yet what is metal but the bones of earth? Without the arrowhead buried in your knee, your body should heal itself. You may lose that limp and have no need to lean on your lady, as you do now."

Vasco straightened. He stayed that way for barely a moment before Bianca managed to get under his shoulder to take some of his weight off his injured leg again. "I am his support as much as he is mine," Bianca declared.

"A little pain wouldn't stop me from protecting my princess," Vasco added, gazing into Bianca's eyes.

It seemed she stood with him in the underwater ballroom again, drawn to one another like moths to the same flame. Yet Vasco's eyes seemed to burn when he gazed her at her, in a way that kindled a strange heat in Bianca's chest.

"Vasco," she breathed, reaching a hand up to his

cheek.

He pulled her hard against him, and kissed her. The fire in her heart blazed, shooting down to curl at her toes. It could burn her to cinders, and she wouldn't care, as long as Vasco didn't stop kissing her.

Several minutes later, Kun's coughing became too alarming to ignore, and they broke off their kiss to stare at the old woman.

"Now, I have other things to take care of." Kun straightened, and it seemed to Bianca that she stood taller all of a sudden. Her hair darkened, too, so that instead of white with strands of black, her hair now looked as sleek as a raven's wing. When she turned around, Bianca barely recognised her. Why, Kun looked younger than her own mother – not much older than Bianca herself. This strange, young Kun laughed, her voice rich and full, without any of the tremors of old age. "Did you truly think me just some weak witch, girl, like your queen? I am an enchantress, gifted in elemental magic, though my affinity has always been with the earth. At the queen's request, for she is my god daughter, for good or ill, I kept those princes prisoner here. I fed them those foolish enough to fall under their spell, or the spell of greed, in the case of those silly boys who saw an easy way to win a wife and property. But they have flown, and my vigil is ended. So, while I thank you for your kind invitation, I will not accept your hospitality at this time. I am needed elsewhere. Perhaps we will meet again, far into the future. My best wishes for your health and happiness, both of you, because I think you two truly have a good chance of living happily ever after."

With that, she traced a fiery circle in the air, stepped through it, and vanished.

Forty-One

Bianca stared after Kun, barely believing her eyes. Then Vasco's arms snaked around her waist, and she could think of no one else but her husband. She turned around. "Kiss me again, just like the first time."

The moment his lips touched hers, desire ignited her whole body once more, and she was surprised to hear her own voice moaning in pleasure.

He broke for breath and grinned at her. "You taste of paradise, princess. But you are wearing too many clothes for my liking." He tugged at the lacing of her gown, which had somehow come undone as they kissed.

She glanced around. "We should go inside for that."

He laughed. "Why? It would be a shame not to use Mistress Kun's wedding gift. And for that, you must be naked."

The hot spring. How had she forgotten?

Vasco stripped off his own clothes, laying them on a rock, then stepped into the pool. Just as she remembered it, his body was all muscle. Once again, she couldn't help staring.

"You may come and touch me instead of just looking if you take your clothes off," he teased.

Her mouth suddenly seemed dry as she fumbled to finish unlacing her gown. She laid it beside his clothes and stood before him only in her shift. "But what if someone sees us? Out here, naked like this?" she asked.

He laughed. "Then you will use your magic to make us invisible. Or I will tell them to go away. This is our estate now, and I am the lord here."

Lord Vasco. She liked the sound of it. Bianca dropped a curtsey, flaring out the hem of her shift. "My lord," she said, pulling the shift off entirely.

Now she found Vasco's eyes on her, devouring her like a starving man might with his first meal. Yet in his eyes, such hunger only inflamed her own.

She stepped cautiously into the water, which now reached just past her knees.

Vasco settled on a natural stone ledge that seemed a

perfectly formed seat for two. He patted the place beside him. "Come sit with me, princess. I want you close enough to kiss."

But Bianca wanted more than a kiss. For a girl who'd lived in a harem all her life, she'd never actually touched a naked man, and she wanted to. She took a deep breath as she crossed the pool, then climbed into his lap and kissed him.

Bianca gasped as she felt him hardening between her thighs. In the harem, the women whispered that if you rode a man just right, he could make your soul take flight. More than anything, she wanted to know what that felt like. She'd tried it on one of the statues in the palace once, but all she'd experienced was pain as she left a smear of blood on the statue's nethers. She hadn't wanted to try again, but with a living, breathing man between her thighs who could turn her whole body to flame with a kiss, she knew it would be different.

She rocked against him, and Vasco groaned. Perhaps they could fly together. She reached down and guided him inside her as she rocked again.

One moment she was empty and aching for him, and the next she was so full of the hard heat of him that she could scarcely breathe. All she knew was she did not want to stop. "More," she gasped.

"Bianca…Bee…" he groaned. "I do not wish to

hurt you. This is your first time. Perhaps we should…"

"You're not hurting me. I want more," she insisted. When still he hesitated, she opened her thighs wider, sliding down his shaft until her knees touched the stone beneath him. She cried out as he filled her completely, revelling in the sheer pleasure of having him inside her as she rode him to heights of pleasure she had only dreamed of before.

All at once, he shuddered into stillness, her name on his lips until she kissed him. Then there was silence, except for their shared breathing and the bubbling of the spring around them. The water had reached her breasts, buoying them up before her.

Vasco stared at her in wonderment. "I feel like a king. No man could ask for more."

Bianca laughed. "Ah, but I am just a princess. As long as you are my husband, I will always want more."

"And I shall always give you what you desire, though perhaps not right away." Vasco kissed her again, long and lovingly, setting the pattern for the first of many nights in their long lives together.

Author's Note

If you're looking for more fairy tale retellings…here's a sneak peek from *Silence: Little Mermaid Retold,* the next book in the series.

Bonus Sneak Peek

Silence: Little Mermaid Retold

The ocean sang in harmony with the oncoming storm. Though she stood on deck, Margareta could hear the song so clearly she wanted to join in. Three times the captain had tried to persuade her to go below decks, or into his cabin at the very least, but she hadn't budged. As long as a single man stood on deck, so would she.

Besides, the cabin was crowded enough with the young prince, his entourage and the cloying reek of seasickness.

She smelled it first, before the fine down on her bare forearms stood on end. Then blinding light erupted from the deck, consuming the mast before splashing across the sky. She clapped her hands over her ears, but it did little to quiet the thunderclap when it came.

After that, silence descended on the ship, for the thunderclap had deafened them all.

When the smoking mast cracked into pieces, smashing through the cabin and all those within, no one heard their screams, or the horrible ripping squeal as the ship's beams broke asunder, surrendering to the sea.

While panicked sailors raced around, trying to put out the fires or save themselves, Margareta sat on the deck and calmly removed her shoes and stockings. There wasn't time for more, as the deck was already awash. The ocean licked at her bare toes, enticing her in.

Margareta climbed over the railing, until there was nothing between her and the waves below. She closed her eyes and dropped, feeling the ocean's cold embrace welcoming her home.

It would be so easy to change into a more suitable form for swimming, and let her mermaid instincts take her to depths where no human could follow, but Margareta resisted. She was supposed to be on the surface, not in the sea. She was the daughter of the Master of Beacon Isle, and Beacon Isle was where she belonged right now.

The island was miles away, and it would be a much easier journey in a boat than relying on her own fins. Maybe one of the lighters had survived intact.

Margareta surfaced to survey the wreckage floating amid the waves. A hatch cover, what looked like a cabin door, barrels, corpses, the curve of an overturned boat...

Smiling, Margareta swam for the boat. A well-placed wave set it right way up. All she had to do was climb in and the ocean would take her home.

She had one hand on the gunwale when she clearly heard someone shout, "For God's sake, help me!" before the words ended in a gurgle.

Among the floating corpses was someone who wasn't dead yet, though he would be soon, if no one helped him. He clung to a splintered chunk of mast that rolled in the waves like a drunken sailor. As Margareta watched, it rolled him under the water before bringing him to the surface again, coughing and spluttering.

"Help!"

Margareta did. Guiding the boat to his side, she reached out to haul him in. He was heavier than she expected, though he was the same size as she, and the boat nearly capsized, but water was her element, so Margareta won him from the ocean.

He flopped into the bottom of the boat, the most unlikely catch ever landed. His fine clothes marked him as one of the prince's entourage, but his gasping mouth made him look more like a fish.

"You're just a girl!" he said.

She was far more than just a girl, but Margareta had more important matters to attend to than educating one of the prince's servants. "I'm the girl who saved your life, and I'd have thought you'd have learned better manners as the prince's pageboy."

"Squire," the boy corrected. "I am…I mean, I was…Prince Philip's squire." He was silent for a moment. "They're all dead now, aren't they? He asked me to fetch them some wine, so I was on deck when the mast crashed into the cabin. It must have crushed them instantly."

Margareta surveyed the corpses, then closed her eyes. "Yes, they are all dead. We are the only ones left, and to survive, we must reach the shore. Do you think you can – "

She should have kept her eyes on the ocean, for she knew how treacherous it could be. One moment they were in the boat, the next a wave sent them tumbling back into the water.

Margareta came up cursing. She'd bitten her lip, so it was with blood on her tongue that she commanded the ocean to do her bidding. The waves brought the boat to her, but the boy was nowhere to be seen. "Find him," she said tersely, ducking under the surface to search for herself.

A glint caught her eye – metal reflecting the lightning above – and she dived, shifting to her tail to give her the power to drag the boy back to the surface. This time, she made the waves lift him into the boat as she hauled herself aboard.

"Take us home," she ordered, and the waves obeyed, parting to form a path before her as a powerful surface current pushed the boat along it.

Satisfied that the ocean would continue to do her bidding without her watching, Margareta turned her attention to the boy. There was no gasping now, nor breathing, either.

"Don't you die on me, squire, or I'll throw you back over the side," she threatened.

No response.

"I saved your life, so it belongs to me, not the ocean. You hear me? No dying on me, now!"

She pounded his chest and back until he coughed up the water he'd swallowed and began to breathe again.

"Who are you?" he croaked out.

"My name is Margareta," she said. "So what's your name, squire?"

"Erik," said the boy. He mumbled something else

that Margareta couldn't quite make out, but before she could ask him to repeat it, he fell back against the boards, unconscious. At least he was alive.

Leaving the stormy ocean in her wake, Margareta's vessel sailed for home.

The tale continues in the next book in the series
Silence: Little Mermaid Retold

About the Author

Demelza Carlton has always loved the ocean, but on her first snorkelling trip she found she was afraid of fish.

She has since swum with sea lions, sharks and sea cucumbers and stood on spray drenched cliffs over a seething sea as a seven-metre cyclonic swell surged in, shattering a shipwreck below.

Demelza now lives in Perth, Western Australia, the shark attack capital of the world.

The *Ocean's Gift* series was her first foray into fiction, followed by her suspense thriller *Nightmares* trilogy. She swears the *Mel Goes to Hell* series ambushed her on a crowded train and wouldn't leave her alone.

Want to know more? You can follow Demelza on Facebook, Twitter, YouTube or her website, Demelza Carlton's Place at:

www.demelzacarlton.com

Books by Demelza Carlton

Ocean's Gift series
Ocean's Gift (#1)
Ocean's Infiltrator (#2)
Ocean's Depths (#3)
Water and Fire

Turbulence and Triumph series
Ocean's Justice (#1)
Ocean's Trial (#2)
Ocean's Triumph (#3)
Ocean's Ride (#4)
Ocean's Cage (#5)
Ocean's Birth (#6)
How To Catch Crabs

Nightmares Trilogy
Nightmares of Caitlin Lockyer (#1)
Necessary Evil of Nathan Miller (#2)
Afterlife of Alana Miller (#3)

Mel Goes to Hell series

Welcome to Hell (#1)
See You in Hell (#2)
Mel Goes to Hell (#3)
To Hell and Back (#4)
The Holiday From Hell (#5)
All Hell Breaks Loose (#6)

Romance Island Resort series

Maid for the Rock Star (#1)
The Rock Star's Email Order Bride (#2)
The Rock Star's Virginity (#3)
The Rock Star and the Billionaire (#4)
The Rock Star Wants A Wife (#5)
The Rock Star's Wedding (#6)
Maid for the South Pole (#7)
Jailbird Bride (#8)

The Complex series

Halcyon

Romance a Medieval Fairytale series

Enchant: Beauty and the Beast Retold (#1)
Awaken: Sleeping Beauty Retold (#2)
Dance: Cinderella Retold (#3)
Revel: Twelve Dancing Princesses Retold (#4)
Silence: Little Mermaid Retold (#5)

www.ingramcontent.com/pod-product-compliance
Lightning Source LLC
Chambersburg PA
CBHW070449120726
47910CB00003B/980